Gleaner

By

Allison Creal

Chapter 1

July 1998

Phillipa Harrison idly swayed her weary body back and forth on a hard plastic kitchen chair, occasionally sipping from a comforting china mug that had been re-filled with freshly brewed herbal tea. As she breathed in the carefully blended heady aroma of lavender, aniseed, bergamot and rosehip, Phillipa listened intently to every word the plump mystical woman sat opposite her was saying. Phillipa Harrison had loyally visited the Medium almost every other day for six months. The tormented woman was seeking comfort and solace following the sudden deaths of her husband and baby daughter in a tragic car accident.

The grieving young mother had been dealt a cruel blow. She had meticulously counted every waking minute of the twenty six weeks, four days and three hours since the bitter twist of fate that had changed the course of her life forever. Phillipa had been driving her family home in her little red Mini on the day of the fatal crash. Even though the traffic collision had not been Phillipa's fault, she still held herself solely to blame for the deaths of her husband Graham and baby daughter Abigail. Phillipa had managed to escape from the mangled wreck of twisted metal with a broken collar bone and fractured arm. She felt immense guilt for having survived the harrowing ordeal and the mournful young mother knew her shattered heart would take far longer to heal than any of her physical injuries.

Now, after six long months of seemingly endless tarot readings, Quija boards, palm readings, auras, tea leaves and visions in crystal balls, the young grief-stricken widow had been drawn back to Carol Frogson's flat on hearing the almost unbelievable news that the Medium said she had finally managed to reach the spirit of Phillipa's dead husband, Graham Harrison.

Carol Frogson had come to know her bereaved client extremely well. She had gently coaxed every facet and fact out of Phillipa. She had soaked up every small detail of her client's life. What her world had been like before the tragic day that had taken away Phillipa's young family. Where she had lived; who she had shared her life with; who she now cried with. Every little thing had been logged in Carol's memory to help her reach the drifting spirits of the dearly departed Graham and Abigail Harrison.

The humble surroundings of Carol Frogson's small, town centre housing association flat were by now a familiar environment to Phillipa. The modest square living room had two large aluminium framed windows at the front with a view of the bustling high street fifteen floors below. A pair of heavy brown dralon curtains had been pulled together across the windows to keep out the invasive summer sunlight. Beneath the window ledge inside this humble room was an old brown leatherette sofa with cracked seat covers and sun-bleached armrests. A chipped wooden coffee table sat in front of the sofa. It had been carefully covered with a black and gold silk headscarf to conceal the damaged surface. On top was a tall engraved church candle that had been infused with incense; its small flame flickered gently in the dimly lit room. Next to it was an old china oil burner that now spat out its last few drops of patchouli vapour into the air. In the corner of the living room was a tiny kitchenette that, although aged, had been well cared for and thoroughly cleaned in anticipation of visitors. There were two internal doors that led off this room, one to a shower room, the other to the only bedroom in the tiny flat.

The two women sat on plastic kitchen chairs at opposite sides of a small square pine table in the centre of the living room. Phillipa felt comfortable in the familiar surroundings of the Medium's home. She firmly believed that if the spirits of her dead husband and baby daughter were going to reach her from the other side, then it would only be through Carol Frogson, her new best friend and psychic confidante.

Phillipa was totally captivated as she breathed in the heady aromas of melting candle wax and the hot scented oil burner. She took another sip of spicy herbal tea and felt its calming steam warm her face. Was this going to be the day? Was this the moment she had longed for? She hoped with all of her lonely breaking heart that this would be her chance to ask Graham to forgive her for driving too fast; to say sorry for not stopping in time when the council bin lorry had jumped the red traffic light; to have a final opportunity to say goodbye to her loving husband and innocent baby daughter.

"Poppy," Carol Frogson had entered a trance. Her eyes were closed, her face expressionless. She tilted her head forward slightly and gripped the edge of the table with both hands, tilting it rhythmically from side to side. Her breathing became deep and laboured. Phillipa eagerly followed every slight twitch of the Medium's lips.

"Poppy. It wasn't your fault," mumbled Carol. Phillipa's heart raced. How good it felt to hear Graham's pet name for her spoken again. A warm glow ignited inside her empty heart and flowed through her body, stinging her chest and flushing her face. Phillipa could feel a fine bead of sweat gently trickle down the side of her right temple; her breathing quickened as her curtain of long curly auburn hair became damp. Was this it? Was this the connection she had been praying for? Would this be her one last chance to make everything all right?

How she had longed to tell Graham the burden of guilt she felt; how she believed she was to blame for the car crash. If only they hadn't been bickering in the car, maybe she would have been concentrating on the road ahead a little more; maybe then she would have noticed the driver of the speeding council bin lorry ignore his red traffic light and set his juggernaut on a fatal collision course with her Mini.

Since that tragic day Phillipa had continually re-lived the fateful seconds when her life had changed forever. During every tormented waking minute she continually churned over the horrific realisation in her mind; the dreadful moment when she knew her loving husband had taken his final breath and her baby daughter's cries had been silenced forever. She had punished herself during every waking hour, hopelessly searching for the chance to say sorry to her husband and little girl. How she longed for the opportunity to explain, to try to atone for her actions. How she ached to make her peace with

3

her family. How she desperately needed their forgiveness. Phillipa's broken bones had healed, but the grief-stricken widow's emotional wounds would never allow her to be at peace until she had been able to contact Graham and Abi to say sorry.

The aroma from the melting scented candle wax filled every inch of the small room; the hot spitting patchouli oil from the burner made Phillipa's green eyes feel sleepy. Her throat was dry as she opened her mouth to speak. She took another sip of spicy herbal tea and pulled away a stray red curl of hair from across her face. She swallowed hard and blinked away a dewy tear.

"Graham, is that you? Darling, is that really you?" she whispered. The Medium's laboured breathing changed to a rasping pant; her head tilted back awkwardly; both hands clutching tightly onto the rocking pine table in front of her.

"Yes, I'm here Poppy," replied the Psychic with a slightly deeper voice. More tears welled up in Phillipa's hopeful eyes as she stared at Carol Frogson's expressionless face.

"Is Abi with you?" Phillipa's voice rose like an excited child's.

"Tell me she's there with you," she squealed.

"Poppy darling, don't worry . . . you weren't to blame . . . " Carol's face still without expression; her voice still deep.

". . . we're together. We're watching over you. We'll be waiting for you. I promise." Carol's deep whispering tone remained steady, almost soothingly catatonic.

"Graham, I'm so sorry, I . . ." Phillipa could hold back no more. She began to cry as fat tears streamed down her hot face. As she struggled to speak, precious memories of her husband and baby girl began to race through Phillipa's mind; meeting Graham at a party, their wedding day, skiing in San Moritz, decorating the nursery, Abi's birthday, holidays, Christmas, getting the keys to her shiny new red Mini . . . the fateful day of the car crash.

Phillipa felt as if her heart was being wrenched from her chest; a creeping stinging sensation violently burning through her whole body. She began to tremble as more haunting memories of the collision flooded into view. The sound of tyres skidding on the damp tarmac; a blasting horn from the truck; a flash of yellow steel as the front of the bin lorry slid uncontrollably closer and closer into view. The devastation of hopelessly shaking her husband's lifeless body in the front passenger seat; the raw terror of seeing Abi's baby seat crushed beneath ribbons of twisted red metal and a shower of broken glass; the torrent of panic racing through her veins as the air inside the car had filled with petrol vapour; passers-by dragging her in slow-motion kicking and screaming from the wreckage. And now, somewhere, in that heady whirlwind of emotion, her brain pulsing with every beat of her heavy thumping heartbeat, Phillipa could hear her little baby Abi crying out in the distance.

"We have to go now Poppy. I love you," the clairvoyant's voice suddenly snapped Phillipa back to cold reality. The Medium let out a long gasp of air as her exhausted body slumped heavily onto the pine table. Phillipa realised that the fleeting precious connection with her young family was shattered once more.

"Get them back! Get them back!" she screamed at Carol. The Medium opened her eyes.

"I can't my lovely, they've gone."

"Get them back! Get them back! Please get them back" begged Phillipa, slamming her hands on the table top. Carol Frogson arose from her plastic kitchen chair. Still feeling a little groggy from her trance, she slowly walked around the table and knelt down beside her sobbing client.

"I'm sorry," she soothed, placing a reassuring hand on Phillipa's trembling arm.

"That's all we can do for today my lovely." She paused for a moment and pulled her seat from the other side of the table. Comforting Phillipa was going to take a while and she needed to take her time. Carol needed to nurture their relationship and build on the trust that Phillipa had in her psychic friend. She drew the chair close and sat beside the grieving young widow.

"You have to remember the spirits are always calling my lovely, they're always out there. It's just that connecting with them takes its toll on me and I get very tired. Perhaps we should try again tomorrow," she offered. Phillipa forced a small but

5

understanding smile back at her friend and slowly nodded her head.

It could have been the heady cocktail of scented candles and spicy herbal tea, but for Phillipa, from that moment on, there was no longer an outside world; there would be no other reality. There was just that precious capsule of time when she had briefly re-connected with her beloved young family. The fleeting conversation with her husband's spirit had ignited the raging fire of hope within Phillipa's soul. But that one moment in time could never be enough. She knew her husband and baby girl were within reach, waiting for her, and somehow she had to find a way to connect with them again. Her friend Carol had undoubtedly forged a strong spiritual bond with the other side, and now Phillipa felt an all-consuming passion to get that contact with her lost family back. For Phillipa without that cherished connection there was no life for her; there was no other reality. There could be no tomorrow. She left Carol's dimly lit flat, her head filled with messages of hope from the dead.

The lift in the block of flats was out of order, so Phillipa began a long trek down fifteen flights of stairs. With each step down Graham's beautifully soothing words twirled around and around inside her mind; his voice becoming stronger and stronger.

'We're together. We're watching over you. We'll be waiting for you. I promise' that's what he had said, that's what Phillipa had heard. Abi in the distance, crying out for her mother's achingly empty arms, that's what she had definitely heard. As she made her way through the shadows and walked down the litter-strewn communal concrete stairwell of Carol's block of flats, Phillipa made the decision that, for her, there could be no life outside of that small room. Her loving husband and baby daughter were watching over her, waiting for her. She knew she had to make contact with Graham and Abi once again, no matter what it took.

Carol pulled back the heavy brown curtains and opened the windows wide. A cool summer breeze flowed through the room, cleansing the air of its heavy stench of incense and patchouli oil. In the distance, as Carol peered out of the window, she could see the gaunt lone figure of Phillipa Harrison waiting at the bus stop fifteen floors below. 'Poor woman,' she thought to herself. 'What must it feel like to have your whole family wiped out like that?'

Carol reached into the pocket of her worn blue jeans and removed the three crisp twenty pound notes that Phillipa had given to her for the reading. 'Poor woman,' a small, wry smile crept across the Medium's lips.

"The spirits are always calling, perhaps we should try again tomorrow," she lightly mocked, fanning her face with the notes as she watched Phillipa step onto a bus. Carol picked up one of the cushions from the sofa, un-zipped its cracked leatherette cover and hastily stuffed one of the twenty pound notes inside. Quickly she re-arranged the cushions before crossing the living room floor to open the door that led into the bedroom.

Carol's husband, Peter Frogson, was sitting at the top of the double divan bed; his head of greasy blond hair propped against a sweat-stained pink fabric headboard.

"She gone then?" he asked, nonchalantly rolling a matchstick-thin joint between his yellowed calloused fingers.

"Yes," replied Carol with a small sigh.

"How much did you get?"

"Forty quid this time," she said, handing him two crisp twenty pound notes. She studied her husband's face, hoping to God that he had believed her lie.

"Well, with any luck she'll be back again tomorrow for more of the same," he sneered, as he snatched the money from Carol's hand.

"Better get this smoked quick then before your next visitor searching for psychic enlightenment comes along," he added with a wry smile

Peter lit his cigarette and inhaled hard. As he lay on his back, letting out a purposeful deep breath of smoke, he passed the spidery joint to Carol but she quickly pushed it away. Kneeling down at the side of a scruffily painted second hand cot, Carol stroked the forehead of her tiny sleeping baby.

Carol hated her life. She loathed her weed-smoking husband and she resented what he had made her become. She was determined to escape the sordid spiral of endless psychic scamming. Her whole life was spent trudging from one squalid day to the next. She funded her small family's hand-to-mouth existence by preying on the vulnerable with her fake messages of hope from the dead. Occasionally she had struck lucky and found long-term believers such as Phillipa Harrison. They were her bread and butter and more rewarding than Carol's other small time hustles. The more she nurtured those relationships, the more sophisticated and believable her readings could become. They were the ones who came back time and time again, begging for more psychic guidance. Unfortunately for Carol, most of her clients would visit only once or twice. Maybe they were less vulnerable and could see through the charlatan's scams; maybe they had just gone along out of curiosity or for a laugh; whatever their reasons it was most ironic that for Carol her income, in fact her whole future, was largely unpredictable.

Carol gazed down at the cot, a small tear rolled from the corner of her eye as she gently picked up her sleeping baby.

"Rest now Emily sweetheart. You were a good little girl today, you only cried out once." She shot an accusing glare at her husband. In Carol's mind Peter Frogson was a useless waste of space. He had one job to do today and that was to keep their baby occupied and quiet during psychic sessions with clients. Any noise coming from inside the flat could affect the atmosphere of a reading. Today he had failed even to do that one simple task properly, as Emily's hungry cry had been heard during Phillipa's visit.

"Don't you worry, Mummy will make it all better for you; you just wait and see," she cooed softly, stifling a small sob into the soft pink fluffy bundle of innocence.

#

Phillipa Harrison made her way home through the afternoon rush hour. The bus began its slow crawl, joining a pulsating snake of stop-start Manchester traffic. With every heave of the engine starting off Phillipa could hear Graham's soothing words; with every squeal of the brakes she could hear Abi's cries. Busy shoppers and commuters jostled for space around her; sullen teenagers bumped into her; grumpy pensioners moaned about the irritating sound of Indie Rock music 'tisk tisking' out of someone's Walkman headphones; but no one noticed Phillipa's sadness. No one saw the pain etched across her white pinched face as she held back grieving tears. No one noticed the desperately unhappy mother leave the bus and quietly walk the short distance to a neat row of terraced houses in Dooley Croft. Phillipa took in a deep purposeful breath and slowly made her way to the driveway in front of number seven. Her tired aching feet carried her past a row of fragrant rose bushes that hugged the edge of a neatly manicured front lawn. She strolled along a colourful flower-decked pathway, before opening a clinically-clean white front door to slip inside the warm serenity of her own home.

No one could have known that within a couple of lonely hours the pale, tired widow with the long curly red hair would drink her final glass of Burgundy wine to wash down the last of her sleeping pills; then take a sheet of lavender coloured velum notepaper and write her tormented farewell message:

I now know Graham and Abi are waiting for me.
Their spirits spoke to me today.
I'm sorry but I have to leave you and be with them.
Please forgive me. Your ever loving sister,
Poppy. xx

Chapter 2

2015 – Seventeen years later –
Timeline: Saturday evening 7pm

Millie Moon sat in her car and turned the ignition key for the third time. 'Whrr whrr whrr.'

"Oh what the fuck is wrong with this sodding heap of junk now," she growled. Millie was angry. She had only recently passed her driving test and that new found freedom was becoming a persistent source of heated arguments between the girl and her over-protective mother. Millie was the only daughter of the celebrity TV Medium, Cellestra Moon.

Millie's parents had reluctantly agreed to allow their feisty teenage daughter to have a car of her own. They had wrongly assumed the novelty of car ownership would soon wear off as their petulant eighteen-year-old would have less money to spend on herself after having to finance it. They assumed that the resulting lack of cash for designer fashions, cocktails and manicures would serve to clip Millie's wings and keep her at home. But they were wrong. Despite the cost, the constant roadside breakdowns, the arguments and the tantrums, Millie loved her new found independence. Not having to rely on lifts from her inquisitive parents was well worth the sacrifice of new clothes and the latest gadgets. Tonight however she was beginning to regret buying the ten-year-old Saxo.

Cellestra Moon had always been highly protective of her daughter. She feared that her strong-minded offspring would choose the wrong friends, go to the wrong places, get in with the wrong crowd or get pregnant by the wrong man. Worse still Millie could easily become the focus of attention of someone who only wanted to be with her because she was an A-list celebrity's daughter. However, it was not just the usual maternal fears that concerned Cellestra. The television Psychic enjoyed a high profile status, but she always felt an uneasy nagging threat lurking at the back of her mind; the feeling that her fame and recently increased wealth could make the TV star and her family a target for all manner of criminals.

Cellestra believed her fears to be totally justified and she constantly warned her daughter to be highly vigilant; but Millie simply dismissed her mother's concerns as over-bearing paranoia. Millie wanted to live a normal teenager's life and couldn't understand why Cellestra Moon was so over-protective and would never willingly let her eighteen-year-old daughter venture out without a chaperone. This had resulted in the cunning feisty teenager becoming highly resourceful when it came to getting her own way.

That evening had been like many others before. Millie had deliberately picked a fight with her mother and they had argued. It was Saturday night and Millie wanted to play. She refused to wait around at the TV studios until 'Cellestra Moon, the country's most adored Medium,' had finished her stage show. Instead Millie had secretly planned to meet up with friends for dinner at The Granary Mill Hotel; that would be followed by a private party into the small hours. The country house hotel was located at the edge of Himley Chase and it had recently become a favourite hang out for celebrities and visiting dignitaries. That evening's prestigious event was to celebrate a local author's book launch and most of the guest list read like a Who's Who of light entertainment; the good, the bad and the ugly. Millie had been given a VIP invitation; just one of the perks of being a celebrity's daughter, and it was something the impressionable teenager simply could not resist. Cellestra had often warned her daughter that there were many people in show business whose sole purpose in life was to take advantage of young naïve girls, but Millie was excited by the thought of mingling with such influential people despite her mother's worries.

In yet another act of teenage defiance, Millie had shouted at the interfering old woman; stroppily slammed shut Cellestra's dressing room door; marched down the corridor and flounced out of the television studios, before crossing the car park to make her getaway. No one was going to stop her from having fun. Millie had timed the whole charade to perfection. She knew her mother could not follow her as she was due on stage within a few minutes to perform for her devoted live television audience. Unfortunately for Millie the finale to this dramatic gesture now lay in tatters and teenage embarrassment, as her car refused to start.

An enraged Millie angrily slammed the steering wheel hard. After several fruitless attempts at starting the engine, she finally admitted defeat, burst open the car door, grabbed the bunch of keys from the ignition and threw them as far away as possible. She felt a huge release of pent up anger leave her body with that one swift throw; as she sent the keys sailing through the air. The full landing force caused the key fob to break; sending tiny splinters of shattered plastic skating across the tarmac. She shook her head and began to clench her fists in frustration, as she realised that she had lost the spat and resigned herself to a boring evening watching her mother's TV show after all. God, how she hated her predictable, mollycoddled life.

"Excuse me luv, d'ya need a lift?" A driver sitting in a pale grey coloured mini cab was trying hard to stifle his laugh. He had pulled up alongside her car when he saw the teenage drama queen's strop. Millie recognised the passing taxi as one from a fleet of courtesy cars contracted to the TV studios. The familiar silver grey hatchbacks were used to ferry around the less important guests and crew members to and from their hotels in the city centre. Although Millie didn't recognise the driver, she knew she would be safe taking a free lift in one of Crucible's cars. Millie was relieved that she had found a new escape route from an otherwise stifling evening with her parents. She hastily gathered up her keys that had become detached from the plastic key fob on the ground and smiled warmly at the man. She eagerly opened the rear car door and edged her way across the scruffy back seat to sit in the middle. Gazing around the interior, Millie wondered if this car would be any more reliable than her own abandoned vehicle. But the temptation to get a free ride on her mother's company expense account, and the chance to salvage an evening of freedom away from her over-bearing parents, was too great.

The taxi driver was a greasy looking man, friendly enough in a chatty small-talk type of way, but a little too lecherous for Millie's liking. However, despite her slight unease about the driver, Millie showed him her studio ID and gave him the

12

address of the country house hotel where she had arranged to meet her friends, before buckling up for the short journey out towards Himley Chase.

"Big night out tonight then?" asked the driver as he punched a postcode into his sat-nav.

"Yes, it's a book launch for a local author so there should be some pretty amazing people there," replied Millie proudly. A small wave of excitement fluttered in her stomach as she thought about the celebrity guest list.

"I don't read many books," quipped the greasy man.

"But I do like my magazines if you know what I mean."

'Fascinating,' thought Millie sarcastically. She imagined the driver's reading habits would be limited to the snippets of news found in lads' mags alongside photographs of scantily clad young women.

"They have some interesting articles about wildlife in them sometimes," he continued.

"Just the other day I read a great thing about tits and cocks." The driver smirked as Millie tried to switch off from what he was saying.

"Yeah, apparently blue tits are one of our most recognisable garden visitors." He laughed childishly, hoping his clumsy attempt at a crude joke would inspire his young passenger to enter into a conversation.

"Now cocks on the other hand, what lady wouldn't like to see a nice big cock in her garden?" Unimpressed by his immature humour, Millie ignored the driver's double entendre and idly gazed around the scruffy interior of the car. She noticed the rear parcel shelf was missing; the thundering noise of the road beneath the car tyres grew louder with every mile. She realised the driver had adjusted his rear view mirror to get a better view of her burgeoning teenage cleavage. His dark eyes periodically darted into view. He appeared to smile excitedly, and Millie noticed his teeth were jagged and stained brown.

'Eugh, what a perv,' she thought.

From the rear seat she could see his hands tapping impatiently on the leather steering wheel. Dirt had gathered around the base of his badly bitten fingernails and the rest of his fingers were grained in what looked like black engine oil. He wore his black curly hair tied back in a short greasy ponytail; his sallow skin looked like unwashed potato peel and, every now and again, Millie caught an unwelcome whiff of the driver's stale body odour.

"How long have you driven for Crucible Cars?" asked Millie in an effort to steer their chatter towards a more mundane topic of conversation; away from his childish jokes about cocks and tits at least.

"Only for a couple of weeks, why?" replied the driver with a quick flash of his brown crooked teeth.

"It's just that I haven't seen you around before," she said, uneasily shifting in the rear seat.

'Don't you even think about chatting me up you horrible little man,' thought Millie, quite repulsed by the idea that the driver might try to keep the conversation going in a vain hope of securing a date with her. Millie reached for a button to crack open the rear passenger window; a vain attempt to get a little fresh air. She quickly discovered the plastic switch casings for both rear windows were broken. Despite clicking the buttons several times, both rear windows remained firmly closed. The driver's body odour was now becoming more intrusive and slightly overwhelming. Millie decided that Crucible Cars' standards had really slipped since she last took a ride in the back of one of their taxis. The cheesy stench of the driver was rather off-putting and such a poor level of service would not give guests of the studio the right impression. Millie would mention it to her mother in the morning; but only after Cellestra had had a chance to calm down after their inevitable argument and forgiven her defiant daughter for sneaking out.

Suddenly the car's engine began to splutter and judder.

"Shit! I knew this would happen," spat the driver under his breath.

"What's wrong?" asked Millie.

"Sorry Miss. It's the fuel gauge. The bloody thing's on the blink. It keeps telling me I've got loads of petrol when really it's running on fumes. Don't worry though I've got a spare can in the boot. There'll be enough petrol in it to get you to the Granary Mill. I'll just pull over down the road a bit."

The driver coasted the car down a hill for a couple of minutes, limping along a deserted country lane, before stopping in a small lay-by on the side of the road. The greasy man immediately sprang out from the driver's seat and skipped around to the back of the car to open up the rear hatch. A welcoming cool summer evening breeze fanned the nape of Millie's neck as the man grappled in the back of the car for the petrol can.

"Here we go then," he said casually, as Millie suddenly felt the weight of a cold steel chain noose pass over her head and pull sharply across her throat. She frantically pulled at the chain but it was now tightly wound around her neck and she couldn't slip her fingers underneath. She heard the heavy clunk of a padlock as the driver secured the other end of the chain to a stowage hook in the boot behind the seat. Gasping for breath Millie tried to scream, but all she could hear was a choking wheeze as the metal dog chain pinched hard into her delicate skin.

"Don't try to escape Miss, they've given me instructions to kill you if you try to escape," hissed the driver through his crooked brown teeth. The wiry man had climbed into the boot space behind the rear seats. Millie could feel his hot stale tobacco breath panting in her ear as he yanked her left wrist into a handcuff and tethered it to the grab rail above the side window. A sickening waft of body odour, beer and cigarettes filled Millie's nostrils. Immediately he wrenched her other flailing hand across towards the opposite side of the car. He tethered her wrist to a short chain that he then handcuffed to the other grab rail.

"Just in case you were thinking of screaming." He took a small crumpled oily rag from his pocket and stuffed it into Millie's mouth before securing it with a length of sticky black duct tape. Quickly the man sprang out of the boot space, slammed the rear hatch shut and returned to the driver's seat. He was about to re-start his engine when Millie suddenly pulled her legs out of the rear foot well. She summoned every ounce of strength that her terrified body could muster and began striking out at her captor. She kicked her legs between the two front seats; jabbing aimlessly into the dusk night air, before managing

15

to lash a sharp stiletto heel across the side of the driver's greasy head.

Despite his small physique, the driver was surprisingly strong. He spun around in his seat and his grainy calloused hands grabbed Millie's thrashing legs. The driver jumped over to squat astride the front centre console as he firmly wedged her kicking ankles under him. Angrily he pulled off her shoes and fired them back at her onto the rear seat. Using more of the sticky black tape he bound her struggling feet together. Finally he had his powerless quarry restrained.

He got out of the car, quickly opened the rear door and reached across her to grab Millie's twitching legs. He grappled with her bound ankles for a moment before pulling them back through the space between the two front seats; forcing them back down towards the floor. Finally, he tethered them with more tape to the bottom of the frame of the seat in front of her.

The greasy man grabbed Millie's handbag from the rear foot well and began turning its contents out onto the front passenger seat. Her small purse, tissues, lipstick, keys and mobile phone spilled out and bounced onto the floor. Angrily the driver grabbed Millie's phone, slapped back into the driver's seat and began to punch a text message into the keypad. After the display screen turned green to confirm the message had been successfully sent, he fired the ignition and eased the car out of the lay-by. Millie realised the mini cab had not broken down; the car had never run out of fuel. It had all been part of the man's evil plan to abduct her.

The driver needed to avoid driving through any brightly lit areas. His sat-nav took him on an unfamiliar route down a maze of winding country lanes. Eventually the car passed through a couple of small sleepy villages, before finally pulling onto a deserted dirt track that led to a local beauty spot called Witches' Wood.

Millie had tried to concentrate on the journey, but attempting to take in any small detail through the tears streaming down her face was hopeless. In the unfamiliar inky darkness all she had seen was a blur of passing trees and hedges. Frightened and alone, tethered to the rear seat of the taxi, Millie could only imagine what harrowing ordeal lay ahead of her. In the cold

16

silence of that terrifying journey Millie could do little more than contemplate her fate. She realised that maybe her over-bearing, over-protective, annoyingly paranoid parents had been right all along; she should have stayed with them. She should have listened. She shouldn't have gone out alone, and now she believed she was going to die. The petrified teenager closed her eyes and did something she had never done in her life before; she began to pray.

Chapter 3

Timeline: Saturday night 9.15pm

"Thank you ladies and gentlemen. It's been an absolute pleasure to help you re-connect with your loved ones this evening. I hope to see you all again soon my lovelies, and remember the spirits are always calling. God Bless you all. Good night."

Cellestra Moon was taking her third curtain call, blowing kisses to the highly charged, insatiable television audience that the celebrity Psychic had effortlessly whipped up into a frenzy of excitement. She had reached the climax of her stage show, and the end of filming for the current series of 'Cellestra, I Can See You'. The highly successful TV series had followed the Medium on the road during her sell-out tour of the UK. This was the final show and editing would begin tomorrow to finely tune the whole tour into a DVD collection of cherry-picked moments that would delight her adoring fans. Tonight had been one of the busiest and best nights she could remember. Cellestra Moon had almost lost count of how many devoted followers in this enthusiastic sell-out television audience had been re-connected with their loved ones in the spirit world. During her exhausting two-hour show the names, places and voices of countless lost souls had just kept coming; grannies and granddads with advice for their descendents; dead children with fond messages for their grieving parents; brave soldiers who had lost their lives in a Middle Eastern war zone giving their loved ones the hope to carry on living without them. Obscure messages meant for 'Bobby, Billy or was it Barry' all got through, and everyone in this awe-struck audience was happy. Even those who were not lucky enough to receive a personal message from the afterlife were happy, as they were invited to try again by returning to another show with Cellestra's trademark sign off:

"Remember, the spirits are always calling."

An excited crowd of devoted fans had flocked around one of the merchandising stands in the foyer. They were all enthusiastically anticipating the arrival of their psychic idol to sign autographs. Cellestra's I Can See You tour had been a phenomenal marketing success. All of the gathered devotees wore their newly purchased tour T-shirts and were clutching copies of Cellestra's previous DVD close to their happy hearts; many of them wore Cellestra Moon rose-tinted glasses, another heavily promoted money-spinner available for loyal followers to purchase from the range of official souvenirs. Amid a flurry of cheers and almost child-like squeals of joy from the waiting crowd, a smiling Cellestra emerged gracefully through the stage door. Cellestra knew that her carefully stage managed piece of theatre didn't stop when the curtain fell. She was still 'on duty,' as she took in a deep breath to prepare for the meet and greet session.

Cellestra Moon looked quite ordinary; like any other over-weight middle-aged woman. Her portly rounded body wore a loose-fitting knee-length blue floral dress; this was complemented by a single string pearl necklace that hung closely around her plump neckline. Two matching pearl and diamante stud earrings glinted beneath her short but softly styled ash blonde hair. Cellestra knew how to behave; her well-rehearsed demeanour under-stated; her smile warm and friendly. She knew how to maintain the love of her loyal fans.

Unknown to her band of happy followers, Cellestra's ordinariness had always been carefully manipulated. Her outwardly natural demeanour was supported by an army of stylists with expensive foundation garments, hairdressers and speech writers; all busily working behind the scenes, twenty-four-seven, to maintain the illusion of normality and keep brand Moon alive. To her devoted fans Cellestra was just an everyday woman that they could easily relate to; someone they could trust. Her wise words sent from the spirits may have been tinged with a slight Mancunian accent, but she always gave it to them straight. They believed there was no pretentious celebrity here; just an honest-talking lass from a Lancashire mill town who understood the common man and woman completely. To her believers Cellestra was just like them; a wife, a mother; an

19

ordinary woman but with an extraordinary gift. They desperately needed to believe that she was their genuine ray of northern sunshine that could bring back hope and joy to their empty lives. Brand Moon always delivered.

The carefully choreographed meet and greet session saw the Medium chat happily with her most loyal followers, posing for photographs, signing their merchandise and accepting flowers and numerous small gifts. Maximum exposure was the order of the day; the more fans Cellestra was able to 'touch' the better. However, it was a difficult balancing act to keep the meet and greet signing sessions to the right length with each person. If one fan was taking up too much of Cellestra's precious time, they were quickly but gently ushered aside by her manager and devoted husband, David Moon.

All fans looked pretty much the same to Cellestra. No one would remember seeing the be-spectacled auburn haired woman who handed over a small lavender coloured package. Her pale white face had been lost amid the sea of printed publicity photos, DVDs, promotional T-shirts and bobbing rose tinted glasses that had gazed back adoringly at the celebrity clairvoyant.

The present from the red head had been graciously accepted by the Medium and swiftly handed over to David Moon who had unceremoniously placed it in the gift collection sack. It had then been dutifully delivered to the Psychic's dressing room, where it now lay in wait; perched on top of a mountain of fluffy teddy bears, lovingly hand-made chocolates and fragrant bouquets of flowers. It was a small, oblong parcel that had been carefully wrapped in lavender coloured velum notepaper and tied with purple floristry ribbon into an elaborate bow. It looked like any other gift from an adoring fan; a small token of appreciation; a hand written note to convey their thanks for Cellestra Moon's good work perhaps. But this small, anonymous package was about to completely rip apart the carefully stage-managed life of the country's most adored Medium forever.

#

The silver Crucible Cars' taxi had eventually stopped at the centre of a small clearing, deep at the heart of Witches' Wood. The driver switched off the engine. Millie stared out into the night. All she could see were intimidating trees, their branches dancing high above her; all she could hear was her own heartbeat thumping through her terrified body. The greasy haired driver cracked open his door and a cool summer breeze fanned through the car. He took a crumpled pre-rolled cigarette from his shirt pocket and lit it with a mauve coloured lighter. In the flickering light of the flame Millie could just make out a faded logo printed on the side of the lighter; a gold-coloured top hat with some black writing beneath. Suddenly the flame was gone and the driver turned around to breathe out a choking plume of smoke directly into Millie's tear-filled eyes.

Suddenly, at the opposite side of the clearing, Millie saw the headlights of an approaching car. Her heart began to race. Was it someone coming who could save her? Maybe it was a courting couple visiting the wood to finish off a romantic evening with beer and chips and a quick fumble in their car.

'Please God, please let them see me; please Jesus let it be someone who can help me,' prayed the petrified teenager.

The approaching car stopped beneath the trees and flashed its headlights a couple of times. The greasy taxi driver signalled back with a single flash. Almost immediately two masked men leaped from the opposite car and made their way to each side of the mini cab, simultaneously opening the rear doors. The driver released Millie's ankle bindings as the other men wrenched her legs apart and re-tethered each foot at opposite sides of the car with nylon cord. She could hear a rasping breath from one of the men as he struggled to secure the length of plastic rope. He started to cough before quickly reaching inside his jacket pocket for an inhaler. Suddenly she felt a cold steel blade slide over the delicate skin of her forearm as the other masked man ordered the driver to cut off Millie's jacket, blouse and skirt. She concentrated hard on her assailants, taking in the smallest detail possible. It was then she noticed the man who had brought the knife spoke with a menacing lisp.

The two masked men slammed the car doors shut and walked to the front of the mini cab. Millie tried to hear what

21

they were saying as she could tell they had begun to argue, but her focus on the two shadowy figures was interrupted, as the taxi driver seized his opportunity to quietly crawl on top of her. His grimy hands shook excitedly as he cut through the sleeves of Millie's jacket, his hot stale breath panted into her ear before he slid his rasping tongue up and across her cheek and down her neck. He ripped open Millie's blouse and roughly pulled down her bra straps to reveal her trembling breasts. He paused for a second as if momentarily fascinated by the terrified teenager, before plunging his head onto her chest to lick his tongue hungrily across her burgeoning cleavage. Millie felt the cold steel blade across her thigh as he furiously tore into her skirt and began to eagerly pull away at the rest of her clothes. Millie let out a sudden stifled cry as the car began to rock from side to side. Suddenly one of the car's rear doors flung open and the asthmatic masked man grabbed the driver by his hair and dragged him out onto the ground.

"What the fucking hell d'ya think you're doin, you wanker?" rasped the man. The startled driver wriggled on the grass in the moonlight.

"I warned you he'd be fuckin' scum," hissed the other man with the lisp, his voice slightly softer yet at the same time more sinister.

". . . you know you're at the end of the fuckin' queue when it comes to playing with the merchandise, you filthy retard," spat the second man.

The wheezing masked man began to cough again as he stood behind the driver and grabbed his oily ponytail, violently pulling back his head. The other man swiftly kicked him hard in the stomach with his steel toe capped boot. The driver groaned in agony and slumped over onto the grass clearing.

"You're a fuckin' snivelling waste of air," jeered the softly spoken lisped voice.

". . . what are you?" he hissed, grabbing the driver under the chin before snatching him to his feet. A small flash of metal glinted in the moonlight as the masked man pulled a knife from his leather ankle holster.

"A a w-w-aste of air," faltered the driver breathlessly, feeling a sharp scratch of glinting steel press into his sweaty groin.

"Again!" demanded the menacing whisper.

"A waste of air. I'm a waste of air," cried the trembling man on feeling a warm trickle of blood ooze down his inside leg.

Millie could hear the terror in the greasy driver's voice. What the hell were they going to do? Her hands and arms were now feeling numb from being tethered to the grab rails; the muscles in her legs burning and tired from her futile attempts to free her feet from their bindings. She tried to cry out, to try to stop what was unfolding before her terrified eyes, but the oily rag taped in her mouth stifled her petrified screams. Millie was powerless as she watched the two masked assailants outside the car taunt their terrified accomplice in the woodland clearing.

Suddenly a tortured gurgling scream pierced the still night air before the driver's lifeless body slumped to the ground.

#

Cellestra and David relaxed in the serene surroundings of the celebrity Medium's dressing room. It was just coming up to midnight and they were giggling and joking like naughty teenagers. The couple had just popped open their third bottle of Cristal Champagne, as they started to plough through the collection of cards and goodwill messages from Cellestra's army of adoring fans.

"How were things with Millie tonight?" asked David casually as he took another gulp from his Champagne flute.

"Oh you know that moody mare," replied Cellestra.

"She's always got to be the bloody centre of attention," she snorted.

"Did you two have another row?" asked David, waiting to hear his wife's predictable list of things that Millie had said and done to annoy her that evening.

"She flounced off in another strop after I asked her not to go out alone in that bloody car of hers," whined Cellestra.

". . . and the little cow timed it all to perfection too; just before I was about to go out on stage and do the show, so I

23

couldn't very well go running after her could I?" David chuckled to himself as he was able to predict almost word-for-word what Cellestra would say next.

"I know she can be difficult sometimes Ce, but she just needs to find her own feet in the world. She's only testing the boundaries you know," he said supportively.

"Besides, she's only gone to that book signing thing at the Granary Mill with some friends," he continued. Cellestra looked back at him quizzically as she re-filled her Champagne flute; it was the first time she had heard about the prestigious event.

"Millie texted me earlier, just before your show finished, to say she was having fun. She'll probably come back tonight full of apologies and the two of you will kiss and make up as usual. She's only testing you Ce," he added with a smile.

"She's such a bloody Daddy's Girl," snorted Cellestra.

"One word from me and she does exactly as she pleases." David smiled back at his wife and shook his head. Cellestra always played the Daddy's Girl card after she'd had an argument with Millie.

"After all we've done for her. One day she'll learn though . . . mark my words," added Cellestra, before finishing off the bubbly contents of her glass.

The Medium's dressing room was comfortable yet functional. It was a peaceful haven away from the hustle and bustle of celebrity life and provided Cellestra and David with a sanctuary away from the outside world. It was a useful bolt-hole for the couple and their daughter, as Millie also had her own small bedroom a little further down the hallway. The family often stayed at the studios overnight during filming rather than commuting to and from their house in the country.

Two large cream leather sofas sat at opposite ends of Cellestra's dressing room; a very heavy, plush cream rug lay in between. Along one wall was a sleek, mirrored wardrobe that neatly stored the Medium's sparkly stage clothes. A 50 inch plasma TV screen almost filled the wall opposite on one side of the narrow room. A large wide dressing table sat beneath the TV screen. It had been laid out with a freshly delivered Champagne supper for two and all of the gifts collected at the stage door. Two elegant Regency style cream leather chairs were neatly tucked beneath the dressing table. At the far end of the room was a door into an en-suite shower room. This sumptuous haven bore testament to Cellestra's phenomenal success; a far cry from her humble beginnings in that tiny Manchester housing association flat; memories of which had been banished to the furthest recesses of her mind many years before.

Carol Frogson had managed to escape the drudgery of married life with Peter sixteen years previously. She had secretly saved enough money from selling psychic readings to enable her to leave her drug-pedalling husband and start a new modest life in the countryside a hundred miles away. A year or so later she had built up a new list of clients within the village she had fled to, and she became a regular attraction at events held by the local Women's Institute. It was at a WI fundraising dinner party where the recently divorced, seemingly respectable Mrs Frogson had been introduced to local accountant David Moon. Following a whirlwind romance they had married and settled down as a family; with Carol's daughter Emily being given her new step-father's second name. With David Moon's guidance and support Carol was set to forge a successful career as a professional Psychic. The old dowdy Carol Frogson was now a shiny new re-born Cellestra Moon. With a new name she had successfully re-invented herself.

With her new husband managing her career, she had swiftly progressed from selling scam psychic readings in her own humble home to receiving clients in the more upmarket surroundings of a private psychic studio. Word of Cellestra Moon's abilities had quickly spread throughout her new neighbourhood; the town and then the county. Soon she was filling village halls and small theatres throughout the middle of England; entertaining the crowds with her amazing insight and contact with the spirit world. Together, with the devoted David firmly at her side, the Moons had built a small psychic empire and within a decade Cellestra's credibility had earned her the recognition as the country's most adored Medium. Psychic insight and paranormal activities were the new rock 'n' roll; the squeaky clean re-branded Cellestra, David and Millie Moon had now become a TV celebrity family.

Cellestra truly believed that she deserved to reap the rewards of her magnificent effort. She would not allow any memories of the small dismal flat that she had once shared with her junkie first husband to spoil it. She would never allow herself to think about the mistake her marriage to Peter Frogson had been, or how she'd managed to secretly save enough money to leave the squalor of his dirty little drug-fuelled world behind.

The young Carol Frogson had planned her escape to a new life very well. One night whilst her husband lay sleeping in another drunken stupor, Carol had bundled up her secret cache of crumpled bank notes from out of the leatherette sofa cushions and stuffed them into the lining of Emily's papoose baby carrier. She pulled a carefully packed rucksack from beneath the bed. Nervously she had slipped on the bag, scooped Emily up into the carrier and quietly tip-toed out of the flat; gently clicking the front door closed behind her. Carol had raced down the rubbish strewn concrete stairway as fast as her legs would carry her, before spilling out onto the busy high street fifteen floors below and running away as furiously as the northern wind blew.

Carol had filed for divorce as soon as she felt she had safely managed to escape the clutches of Peter Frogson. From the sanctuary of a women's refuge she had been more than willing to give the police all the ammunition they needed to secure her estranged husband's conviction for drug dealing. On the first day of Peter's trial Carol was granted sole custody of their baby daughter. On the first day of Peter's ten-year prison term, Carol vowed from that day forward she would never look back.

She was a different woman now. Any memories of that squalid episode that tried to bubble up to the shiny surface of Cellestra's new life were well and truly banished. Even her daughter Emily had been re-branded with a funky shortened first name, Millie. Peter Frogson had been left to rot in a cell and he would never be allowed to infect their lives again.

Cellestra sighed contentedly as she watched David Moon inspect the mountainous hoard of gifts on the dressing table. The Psychic had become used to receiving large numbers of presents from her fans, and over the years had become spoiled and ungrateful. Occasionally she became a little tired of opening endless boxes of Belgian chocolates, designer perfume and hand-crafted teddy bears. To relieve the boredom of such predictable gifts and trinkets, she had invented a small game that she played with her husband, in which they would take it in turns to guess the contents of the packages in front of them.

"This is a bit different" said David, giving an oblong lavender coloured package a gentle shake.

"Oooh, yes. I wonder if it's really expensive chocolate?" replied Cellestra with a wry smile.

"Stop it!" scolded David, playfully.

"You shouldn't take your fans for granted you know . . . after all they can't help being delusional," he laughed, passing the small and beautifully wrapped package over to Cellestra's eager grasp.

"Oooh, it feels a bit different" said Cellestra, as her pudgy fingers began to pull at the ribbon bow and un-wrap the delicate paper.

"There's something rattling inside this box," she squealed in excitement.

"Gosh, I really hoped it was going to be more Belgian chocolate" she said sarcastically.

Opening the plain white card box inside Cellestra discovered a pay-as-you-go mobile phone and a letter. Suddenly her laugh evaporated as she read a few lines of text printed on the sheet of lavender velum notepaper inside the parcel.

If you ever want to see your daughter alive again, use this mobile phone.

Text YES to the number stored in the list of contacts.

Then wait for an important call. Do not switch the phone off.

Do NOT tell the Police about this. You have been warned.

\#

Timeline: Saturday night, midnight

The two masked men had returned to the taxi, and now sat silently in the front seats. The man in the driver's seat had his arm out of the open window and was impatiently tapping the roof of the car with a mobile phone. The other man kept silent

27

watch over their terrified quarry on the rear seat. Millie's heart raced, faster and faster; she felt as if she could literally hear her blood pounding through her brain. She could see from the clock on the dashboard that almost three hours had passed since the driver had met his fate in the grass clearing. 'What are they waiting for?' 'What are they going to do next?' she thought as she stared out of the window at the motionless body on the ground. 'Had they really killed the man in cold blood?'

The asthmatic man in the front passenger seat wheezed as he casually leaned against the window post and took a cigarette from a carton in his left coat pocket. He let out a rasping cough as he raised the cigarette to the slit mouth opening in his balaclava. His mauve and gold cigarette lighter sparked into life. Millie blinked her eyes as the masked man turned around to tauntingly breath out little circles of smoke over the back seat of the car.

'I hope the wheezy bastard chokes to fucking death,' she thought.

Suddenly the kidnapper's mobile phone bleeped and its screen lit up, brightly illuminating the dark interior of the car. The man with the phone nodded his head at his accomplice, and pressed a button on the display to dial a saved number.

"Hello?" asked a quivering woman's voice at the other end of the line.

"Is that Cellestra Moon?" whispered the man with the lisp. Millie jolted with fear on the back seat of the car.

"Yes," replied the Medium nervously.

"Listen very carefully Carol," spat the man with a slightly rolled R at the middle of her name. Millie noticed his head twitched nervously from side to side when he spoke.

The asthmatic smoking man reached over the back of his seat and ripped the black sticky duct tape away from Millie's face, pulling the wet greasy rag out of her mouth. She started to scream. The sound of her own heartbeat thundered through Millie's head. She wriggled around on the back seat screaming out for her mother, pulling and tugging at the bindings with every ounce of strength left in her burned out muscles; but deep down she knew her efforts would be in vain.

Cellestra froze with fear; the whisper of her old name sent a shock of electricity stinging through her heart. The moment she had dreaded most had now caught up with her; someone had taken her baby girl. The muffled sound of Millie's stifled cries could still be heard in the background as the softly spoken voice continued.

"If you want to see your daughter alive again you must correctly predict all six winning numbers on next Saturday's Shimmer Stakes lottery draw. You will text this mobile phone at least twenty-four hours before the draw and tell me what the numbers will be. You will then get your husband to buy a lottery ticket. If your numbers are correct and you are successful, then you will use the winnings to pay the ransom to get your daughter back. If you fail to predict the numbers you will be exposed as the fraud we all know you are and you will lose your daughter. Is that clear?" There was a short pause.

"Do you understand?" demanded the sinister lisping voice on the phone. Cellestra felt as if her life's blood was draining out of her body and into her shoes.

"Yes," she quivered.

"Oh, and one other thing Carol," Cellestra felt dizzy and needed to be sick.

"Just like it says in the note; don't even think about going to the police. If you do, then the deal's dead."

The man hung up the phone and nodded to his accomplice. They both got out of the taxi and opened the rear doors of the car. One of the masked men secured Millie's wriggling left arm in a wrestling hold as the other took out a pre-loaded hypodermic syringe from his coat pocket. She was powerless to escape the sharp stab of the needle, as its hot liquid stung deep into her vein. Millie simply closed her eyes and drifted into darkness.

Chapter 4

Timeline: Sunday morning 1am

A shocked motionless Cellestra Moon sat in cold silence waiting for the police officers to arrive. The lisping voice on the phone had seemed vaguely familiar, but in the tornado of fear that had ripped through her mind on being told Millie had been kidnapped, the frightened woman was unable to place where she had heard the voice before. Despite her begging David not to tell anyone about the kidnapping and ransom demand, her husband had insisted that the only chance they had of getting Millie back would be with the help of the police. Involving the authorities was the right thing to do.

Half an hour later an almost skeletal-looking studio secretary led two plain-clothed policemen through the concrete corridor from the stage door towards Cellestra's dressing room. Teetering at the doorway on a pair of ungainly stiletto heels, the woman raised a small bony hand to knock softly on the door. One of the officers thought the secretary's fragile fingers looked so delicate they were in danger of shattering as she fired a quick succession of taps on the door. Without waiting for a response, the secretary slowly pushed the door open and introduced her suited entourage.

Cellestra was seated at one end of the cream leather sofa furthest from the door, David's reassuring arm around her shoulders. Her ashen face was puffy and her sore eyes were red from crying. Thick smudges of mascara trailed down each plump rosy cheek as she continued to stare into the distance. As if frozen in that small capsule of time, Cellestra's hands still clutched the mobile phone and lavender coloured notepaper tightly to her chest.

"Ms Moon, these two gentlemen are police officers," said the gaunt-looking secretary, trying to break the awkward silence in the room without intruding on what was obviously a tense and private moment.

"I'm Detective Inspector Richens and this is Detective Sergeant Duke, we're from Hanford CID," announced the taller of the two men, as they both brushed past the secretary and entered Cellestra's dressing room. Sergeant Duke nodded a small acknowledgment of thanks to the woman before firmly closing the door behind them.

Cellestra remained motionless, still clutching the mobile phone; still holding on to that last precious moment when she had heard Millie's voice cry out in terror. Detective Inspector Richens gently pulled out one of the Regency leather chairs from beneath the dressing table and placed it carefully to sit down next to Cellestra. He had been fully briefed about the incident in the car on the way over from the police station, but he was keen to get what he called a 'feel' for the case; a gut reaction to events. That could only be gained from talking to the person at the eye of the storm.

"I know how hard this is for you Ms Moon, but the best chance we have of finding your daughter is if we act promptly and follow up any information you can give us at this early stage; anything at all. What can you tell me about the voice on the phone Ms Moon?" asked Richens softly. Slowly the policeman took a deep breath and brought the palms of his hands together. He raised his index fingers towards the fine pointed tip of his thin nose and tucked both of his thumbs beneath his stubbly chin. Duke watched him adopt what had become known back at the station as Richens' prayer pose.

"Did you recognise an accent of any kind?" coaxed Richens. Cellestra continued to stare silently into the cold and hazy distance.

Detective Sergeant Duke listened to his boss gently start his interview, as he surveyed the star's dressing room. A pile of un-opened cards and small gifts were stacked high at one end of the dressing table next to a couple of empty Champagne bottles. Numerous boxes of half sampled Belgian chocolates lay open, strewn across the two empty dinner plates that were smudged with the discarded remains of a luxurious supper. On the far wall above one of the cream leather sofas were framed newspaper cuttings, reviews and photographs of Cellestra Moon. Sergeant Duke noticed how these had all been carefully

31

arranged in strict chronological order, behind a spotlessly clean sheet of glass; an accurate timeline that charted the Medium's spectacular rise and glittering show business career.

"Was there anything unusual about the voice?" continued Richens patiently, trying to squeeze a response from Cellestra's blank expression.

"I'm sorry Inspector," interrupted David Moon.

"The studio Doctor's given my wife something for the shock. I think she might be more up for talking after she's rested." Inspector Richens checked his watch for the time before scribbling down a few sentences. As he rose from the dressing table chair he folded away his notepad and Cellestra slowly lifted her head towards him.

"Oh God," she cried out.

"No one must know . . . he said no one must ever know." Cellestra's eyes welled up with yet more tears.

"He said not to go to the police or the deal's dead."

Panicking, Cellestra suddenly got up from the sofa. Still clutching the mobile phone and piece of lavender coloured notepaper close to her pounding chest, she began to pace around the small dressing room, switching from one end of the room to the other; turning purposefully whenever she reached one of the cream leather sofas at each end of the rug. Breathing deeper with each stride, the phone and notepaper rose and fell with every breath of her heaving bosom. Suddenly she stopped, turned around and used the phone to point accusingly at her husband.

"What the hell have you done?" she screamed. David jolted back onto the sofa, startled by Cellestra's outburst.

"Millie is my fucking daughter," she snarled, jabbing at her own chest with the closed fist that held the lavender notepaper.

"She's mine, not yours. What right did you have to call in the bloody plod you idiot?" she sobbed.

"You know how rumours fly through this place like a fucking wild fire," her eyes aflame now with anger.

"All it'll take is for that anorexic Annie in the stilettos to start blabbing that she showed a couple of coppers to my dressing room door, and it'll be all over the fucking papers tomorrow. I'll be finished David, don't you understand? Finished," she raged.

David sprang up from the sofa and grabbed Cellestra around the shoulders.

"Stop it! Stop it now!" he shouted, firmly shaking her.

"We agreed, telling the police was the only thing we could do Cellestra. For God's sake woman, see sense will you. How the hell would we ever deal with something like this on our own?"

Inspector Richens glanced over to his Sergeant, as Cellestra now clung onto David. She began sobbing uncontrollably into the warmth of her husband's chest. Richens' eyes darted towards the door and then back to his Sergeant; a familiar, well-choreographed signal that it was time for DS Duke to leave the room.

"Ms Moon. We are as anxious as you are to see the safe return of your daughter," soothed Inspector Richens.

"I'm not going to allow anything to affect that," his well-rehearsed manner reassuringly calm and apparently unaffected by Cellestra's emotional outburst. He smiled at the tearful woman who was now sniffing back hiccups.

"You just tell me everything that you can remember about the phone call and . . ." Richens took a deep purposeful breath.

"My sergeant here will go and speak to the staff. I promise the kidnapper will never know you contacted us."

#

Timeline: Sunday morning 5am

Millie awoke from her drug fuelled sleep and slowly blinked open two swollen eyes to take in her new unfamiliar surroundings. She had been taken to an industrial unit. The damp, motionless air inside the factory smelled of cellulose paint and metal filings. The concrete floor was caked in a thick black film; the legacy from decades of endless engine oil changes. Every surface was dusted with fine shards of metal and glass. A dull shaft of daylight found its way through a large gaping hole in the corrugated iron roof and dimly illuminated

33

the space below. An excited group of rats squeaked and jostled for pole position around some dried breadcrumbs left over from a packed lunch; its stale crusts and cellophane wrapper recently discarded. An industrial band saw droned continually in a nearby unit, as squealing pieces of metal were fed through the non-relenting sharpened teeth of its blade. Heavy condensation clung to the slimy brickwork. It was the dawn of a new day and Millie wondered if it would be her last.

The terrified teenager flinched as a droplet of stagnant water landed on her neck and trickled down between her shoulder blades. She peered down and was shocked to see she had been stripped to her underwear and propped up against a clammy wall. She was sitting on the cold factory floor with both legs straight out in front of her. Both wrists were firmly secured together behind her back. Millie's ankles, knees and thighs had been tightly bound with thick black duct tape and then tied to a narrow wooden pole, preventing her from bending her knees. A saliva soaked rag filled her mouth, held in place with more duct tape. Millie had been dragged across the floor of this soulless place and her once wispy fine blonde hair was now matted and hung stiffly around her shoulders; the foul stench of engine oil clung heavily to each strand.

Slowly the hazy recollection of the previous night's ordeal began to fill her brain; the greasy driver, the country lane, the two masked men; the phone call to her mother. It all seemed so surreal, had it been an awful dream? But as she looked down at her dirty panties and snagged bra there was no escaping the grim reality that she was in a perilous situation.

From the corner of her vision she realised that the group of rats had cut short their opportunistic feast and all of their small beady eyes were now focused on her; watching her every move. She could hear their squeaking chatter and the patter of their feet, as they moved like a wave of black and brown fur, scuttling across the concrete floor towards her. Paralysed with fear, Millie closed her eyes tightly and screamed into the gagging rag, her heart beat pounded louder and louder through her brain. But it was useless. Her terrified shrieks were muffled; no one would hear her frantic cries. After a moment she could no longer hear the animals' jostling squeals. Millie bravely opened one eye and then the other, trying to see how close the rats were. She was relieved to see they had been drawn towards another source of food at the opposite end of the factory unit and the colony was thankfully pre-occupied for now. Millie tried to focus and take in the shockingly unfamiliar environment. Where was she? Was she alone with only the gnawing rodents for company? She shuffled forwards, away from the wall, to escape the chill of dripping condensation. Suddenly a sharp throttling tug stopped her. Letting out a short muffled scream she rolled her head around. Staring upwards she could see a length of nylon packaging twine attached to a large metal ring in the slippery wall behind her; this was tied to a rope noose around her neck that now felt like it burned into her delicate skin. Sobbing in the sheer terror of what her fate may hold, Millie collapsed back against the wall and shivered.

#

"So Duchess, what d'ya reckon to the Psychic and her side kick?" asked Inspector Richens irreverently, as he briskly crossed the car park of the TV studios.

DS Duke hated the Duchess nickname that his boss was so fond of using. To DI Richens this was just a term of endearment among colleagues, a tension release, a bit of friendly coppers' banter. To DS Duke it felt like a bullying challenge to his masculinity and it grated on his nerves each time he heard it. Fortunately no one else at the station used it to his face, as Duke would have ignored them anyway until they addressed him properly. But Richens was his senior officer and as such got away with many irritating habits.

"Hard to say," replied Duke thoughtfully.

"I couldn't help feeling . . ." he paused, searchingly scratching his chin and rolling his eyes to the sky as if seeking Divine intervention.

"What?" asked Richens impatiently.

"Well sir, from what I heard, I couldn't help feeling that Cellestra Moon was more upset at the prospect of her reputation being damaged, than she was about the possibility of losing her only daughter."

Following her emotional outburst in the dressing room, Cellestra had eventually calmed down sufficiently to give DI Richens a detailed account of the telephone conversation with her daughter's kidnapper. She had described the man's voice as being small and softly spoken with a lisp. It sounded almost effeminate and he occasionally pronounced the letter R as a W. The Psychic had repeated her edited version of the chilling whispered threats; carefully erasing the name Carol Frogson from her suitably adjusted recollection. Cellestra had cried when she described hearing her daughter's screams in the background. The woman's fear and torment had been clear to see.

"I know what you mean," said Richens. "I got the feeling that she seemed more bothered about how she would be portrayed when it came out in the press. And another thing Duchess . . ." Sergeant Duke flinched at the annoyance of his nickname.

"You'd think an insightful Medium like her; with an undoubted connection to the other side . . ." a wry smile began to creep across Richens' leathery face.

". . . you'd think she would be prepared to at least try and predict a few lottery numbers to save her daughter's life wouldn't you." Richens couldn't help feeling that Cellestra Moon was holding something back.

"Hmmm," agreed Duke reaching into the boot of the police car for a pack of polythene evidence bags.

"The old chestnut of not being able to use her 'gift' for her own personal gain all seems a bit lame to me sir," continued Duke, as he caught site of a promotional poster for Cellestra's sold out show.

"If she's so bloody good at her job, how come the country's most adored Medium was so afraid to give it a go and predict the weekend's lottery numbers?" The sarcasm in Duke's voice was clear.

"Who knows Duchess? Maybe she couldn't 'channel her energies' due to the pressure she's under," smirked Richens, raising his hands in the air to give a mocking inverted commas motion. The inspector picked up a roll of blue and white incident tape from a box in the boot of his car.

"I'll nip back to the nick and see if forensics can come up with anything off this piece of notepaper left by the kidnappers. You stay here and make sure the scene is properly secured," said Richens as he passed the roll of tape to Duke before getting into his car.

Cellestra had eventually let go of the crumpled lavender sheet and given it to Richens. He had carefully placed it inside a self-sealing polythene evidence bag to be taken back to the police lab and scrutinised. It seemed clear to both of these sceptical men that this case would not be resolved by psychic intervention; they agreed that the country's most adored Medium had about as much chance of correctly predicting the winning lottery numbers as they had.

#

Timeline: Sunday morning 6am

Millie shuddered as another slither of chilling water ran down the nape of her neck. Questions raced through her mind. How long had she been here? What was going to happen to her? Would she ever see her parents again? When would she die?

"Hello Emily," a softly spoken voice echoed from the shadows.

Millie tried to let out a scream, the oily rag in her mouth still firmly held in place. She tried to track where the whisper had come from, but she was finding it more and more difficult to breathe. With each move away from the wall, the noose around her neck tightened, burning into her raw skin.

"Where's your mummy now Emily?" taunted the voice.

"I'm NOT Emily, I'm Millie" she screamed into the gagging rag, but no one wanted to hear her protests.

"Emily, Emily, your mummy's a fraud," chanted the echoes in a weird sing-song melody.

"Your mummy's a lying, cheating fucking con artist Emily, and pretty soon everyone's going to see her for the nasty piece of shit she really is," the sinister voice getting closer now.

'Oh God, he's got the wrong girl and I'm going to die' thought Millie, catching sight of a shadowy figure which was

37

skipping about and moving closer towards her trembling body. 'He's got the wrong fucking girl and I'm going to die just like that man in the woods.'

"Let's see how your mummy likes it Emily," whispered the voice, slowly closing in. Millie could hear the malevolent excitement in the man's tone.

"Let's see if your mummy likes to receive messages from her dead relatives. Let's see how she likes to be given false hope," the man's hot wheezing breath now deep within Millie's ear.

"No, no, you've got the wrong girl," screamed Millie inside her head, twisting and struggling to break free from the twine.

"Come on Emily, let's give mummy a message from the dead," the voice now raging from above. Millie suddenly felt a hot streak of pain across her face as the black sticky tape was wrenched away and the oily rag pulled from her mouth. Coughing and spitting, Millie let out a choked moan.

"I'm not Emily, I'm Millie. I'm Millie Moon," she panted. The voice returned to the shadows and began to laugh.

"I'm not Emily, I'm Millie" he imitated, with a mocking whimper. Millie blinked at the shadows, her tear-stained face pale and confused.

"You stupid bint," spat the voice.

"Christ almighty," his whispering tone becoming incredulous now.

"All these years and Carol Frogson's even been deceiving you, her own daughter."

"I don't know what you mean," cried Millie.

"Who has been deceiving me?"

"Your fucking mother," bellowed the voice.

"Carol fucking Frogson. Your spiteful, deceiving, fraud of a mother. The selfish liar of a mother who reinvented herself so she could spin more and more of her filthy lies to even more gullible souls."

"No, no, no," screamed Millie into the darkness. Her eyes had become accustomed to the low light but she could still only make out the outline of her captor's figure in the far corner of the building. She caught a glimpse of his balaclava'd face as he flicked open a small flame from his lighter. He took in a long draw to light a cigarette and the hot embers at its end glowed into life. The lung-expanding plume of smoke made the man cough so he took in another breath of air to try and clear his throat.

"That thoughtless fat bitch would stop at nothing; feeding all those poor people false hope, taking their money, spreading her venom, filling their brains with her poison, giving them more lies, taking more money, keeping them coming back for more and more," he ranted, taking small intermittent puffs of his cigarette. Millie followed the shadowy figure with her eyes as he darted about the factory unit, skipping from left to right then back again. He had a peculiar gait when he moved, and she noticed how wheezy the man's verbal tirade sounded; his voice grew more breathless with each angry accusation.

"But you've got it wrong," cried Millie.

"My mother isn't this Carol woman, she's genuine; she's Cellestra and always has been."

"Pha!" snorted the voice. The man let out a sharp cough and took a large gulp of air through what was obviously an inhaler. It was clear to the terrified teenager that he was agitated and fighting to keep his breathing under control.

"Your mother a genuine Psychic?" he mocked, his asthmatic rasps now sounding more menacing.

"Well she never saw this fucking coming did she?" he growled as he loomed over her with a hypodermic syringe.

\#

Cellestra sat alone at the table in her dressing room and slowly took in a deep breath. Detective Inspector Richens had asked to meet her outside, but the Medium was in no mood to speak to anyone. She had slept at the studio and the effects of the sedative that the doctor had given her the night before had worn off. She now felt a headache beginning to build in her temples. Cellestra took the last two Paracetamol tablets from a blister pack in her handbag and swallowed them with a couple of glugs of water. She glared back at her reflection in the TV screen above the dressing table. The tired woman was not happy with what she saw. She picked up a mirror to survey the

39

damage of a fretful night. Her uncombed hair hung scruffily around her plump face; smears of mascara ran down both cheeks and filled the lines and crevices beneath her baggy eyes. Reluctantly she stood up, picked up a cashmere shawl and made her way outside to meet the policeman.

Cellestra stood at the open stage door and stared intently out at the television studios car park as more detectives arrived. Two by two they turned up in white forensics' overalls, donning white polythene hats, latex gloves and wearing elasticated plastic bags over their shoes. Resembling an infestation of giant white ants, their production line had hustled and bustled throughout the night. Now, just after the break of dawn, another policeman, laden with a myriad of cameras, and silver coloured flight cases, strode out of the television studios and onto the car park. He purposefully removed a tripod from one of the flight cases and opened out the legs, before carefully securing a digital camera to the top. He began to photograph every square inch of the ground around Millie's abandoned car. A geeky looking assistant, carrying a case filled with a collection of small plastic bottles, brushes, evidence bags and glass slides followed him around like a loyal puppy.

Two PCs stood on guard at the entrance to the staff car park, turning away any unsuspecting studio employees that had turned up for the day shift. Ribbons of blue and white crime scene tape fluttered in the early morning summer breeze, sealing off the whole area. Large hand-written notices had been hastily taped to the brick walls to explain that employees should find an alternative place to park, as due to 're-scheduled filming' the area was now a closed set until further notice.

Richens finally returned to the scene and greeted his sergeant on the car park. Both men walked towards the building, bending underneath a piece of blue and white police tape that Duke had tied across the bottom of some concrete steps that led off the car park to the stage door. Cellestra shivered as she watched the two men approach her.

"We've managed to preserve the scene, and a truck will come later to take Millie's car away for further examination," said Richens with a slight sniff; the cool morning air had reached his nostrils.

"My Sergeant will make a start on examining all the CCTV images from inside and outside the building for the last seven days." Sergeant Duke looked quizzically at his boss, wondering why he had been the unlucky one chosen for such a mind-numbing task.

David Moon had told the officers that Millie told him she had planned to drive out to a hotel to meet friends at a book signing the previous evening. As her broken down car and shattered plastic key fob were still on the car park they believed she must have been picked up by someone. She had not attended the event, so they needed to establish her last movements and hoped the CCTV would give them details of who she went away with.

Cellestra hugged her purple and gold cashmere shawl closer to her body in a vain attempt to keep out the cold morning air. In her mind she re-played the last conversation she had with Millie before the impetuous adolescent had flounced out of the dressing room. Her thoughts wandered through so many other happier memories of her daughter. She remembered how, as a pretty five-year-old, Millie had sweetly played the part of flower girl at her and David's wedding; she thought how beautiful her daughter had looked climbing into the stretch limo on her school prom night and how every boy in the room had asked her to dance. Tears welled up in Cellestra's eyes as she recalled how thrilled she had been when Millie passed all of her A levels and how secretly proud she was that her feisty teenager had passed her driving test at the first attempt. Despite Millie's difficult start in life, she was blossoming into an independent sensible young lady that any mother would wish to have. Now, the last memory of her daughter could be that of a mindless argument and Cellestra felt sick at that looming possibility. If only she had followed Millie outside; if only she had stopped her leaving the warm sanctuary of her dressing room, surely none of this nightmare would have happened.

She took in a sharp gasp of air as her mind raced back to the memory of the squalid flat she used to share with Peter Frogson; the look of anger and hatred she had seen on his face as she watched two prison guards take him out of the Crown Court a convicted man. He was the one person from her past

41

who had known all of her secrets and scams back then. He had the knowledge that could expose her as a fraud and he had a powerful motive to totally blow her carefully stage managed world apart. Surely he wouldn't use his own daughter as a pawn in his spiteful revenge?

"How are we going to keep this from the press?" interrupted Cellestra.

"You mean this fairground?" replied Richens surprised by her question whilst gesturing at the army of white overalls crawling over the car park.

"Don't worry Ms Moon your husband said he'll take care of any fallout."

#

Timeline: Sunday 8am through to midday

Following numerous frantic telephone conversations into the early hours, David Moon had spent the whole of the next morning in hastily arranged emergency meetings with the board of directors at the television production company. He knew he had to convince the CEO it was of paramount importance that the kidnapper believed the police had not been told of Millie's abduction. The perpetrator needed to think he was in control; he was the one calling the shots. Millie's life may well depend on it.

David had suggested that the TV company was perfectly placed to prevent reports of Millie's kidnapping reaching the media, and therefore keep the kidnapper in the dark. They could easily close ranks and disguise the police activity in the building as filming for a new television crime drama; the police officers could then carry out a thorough forensic investigation of the scene undetected. Any suspicious studio employees would be told that the officers were actors working on a closed set, so the police would be able to continue their enquiries unhindered. The studio executives would start a viral rumour online that Cellestra Moon had a cameo appearance in a pilot for a new fictional crime drama.

The CEO and his small board of directors had reluctantly agreed with David Moon's persuasive plan. After all they had a duty to support the country's most adored TV Medium; her latest show was the biggest money spinner that their production company had ever commissioned. Covering up the police investigation and keeping the kidnapping under wraps would be a challenge, but they had too much riding on Cellestra Moon and too much to lose if her empire fell apart. From now on, as far as anyone who worked at the studios was concerned, filming of the first episode of the unscripted crime drama was underway on the car park, and Cellestra's recent visit from the boys in blue had been part of the show.

Chapter 5

Timeline: Sunday late afternoon
to early evening

DS Duke sat at his desk, staring at an unopened envelope of crime scene photographs that had just been placed in front of him. DI Richens, who had wandered in with a coffee and the local newspaper, began to glance over the accompanying report. A jogger had taken a route through Witches' Wood earlier that day and discovered a small pile of torn women's clothing. The garments had been listed as a ripped beige Chanel skirt suit and cream blouse, a pair of shredded tights, one brown stiletto shoe and a beige clutch bag. A lipstick, small purse, bunch of keys and a mobile phone had been found close by. Another stiletto shoe, with a blood stained broken heel, had lain discarded in a nearby bush. A further search of the area had revealed a dead body in the undergrowth nearby.

"We haven't had the full forensics' report yet," babbled a breathless PC who had hurriedly run up two flights of metal stairs to deliver a follow-up report to CID.

". . . but initial findings suggest that the clothes were cut from a body with a knife sir." Sergeant Duke rubbed a closed hand across the bristles on his face.

"A body? Did the clothes not belong to *the* body found nearby?" asked DS Duke, reaching for the unopened envelope.

"We don't think so sarg," continued the wheezing PC, trying in vain to catch his breath from his impromptu jog upstairs.

". . . because the mobile phone and a debit card found in the purse all belonged to a Miss Millie Moon but the body found in Witches' Wood was an unidentified male. The clothes match the description of ones missing from Miss Moon's wardrobe, so unless the bloke was a burgling cross-dresser, then SOCO reckon there's a good chance the clothes belong to Millie." Duke breathed a sigh of relief as he realised there was still a small glimmer of hope that the kidnapped girl was still alive. The sergeant opened the envelope of crime scene photographs.

"The report says that the coroner's initial examination has found the unidentified man's blood on the heel of the broken stiletto," said Richens as he read the accompanying document.

"And forensics say his finger prints are the most recent on Millie's mobile." The inspector nodded his thanks to dismiss the PC who was hovering in the open doorway, before returning his attention to the typed up report in front of him.

"And get this Duchess; the last outgoing activity on the phone was a text message to David Moon's mobile," announced Richens.

"Hmm, it all strongly suggests the dead man is connected to the disappearance of Millie then," replied Duke, irritated by his boss's irreverent use of his nickname.

DS Duke had spent most of the day reviewing hours of CCTV footage from the television studios. The camera over the staff car park had picked up Millie getting into her car at 7pm, before getting back out of it a few moments later. He could sense the teenager's frustration as she angrily threw her keys across the car park. She had then struck up a conversation with the driver of a taxi cab before getting into the rear seat of his car. That car and driver would be easy to trace and DS Duke had asked one of his CID team to contact Crucible Cars for their employee's details. Duke replayed the CCTV footage and scrutinised the grainy images. The driver of the car was small and wiry with a pony tail. He noticed that he bore a close resemblance to the photograph of the dead man that had been discovered in Witches' Wood.

#

Timeline: Sunday night 9pm

Millie came round from another drug-induced sleep. Blinking open her tired sore eyes she could still sense a figure in the shadows watching over her.

"Did you have a nice little nap Emily?" taunted the voice sarcastically.

45

The oily rag had been stuffed back into her mouth and secured with lengths of black duct tape. She let out a muffled scream, the sound of her own terror filling her head. Millie could see the glint of a cold steel blade approaching from the darkness.

"You know your mummy can't save you now Emily." The sing-song whisper and the knife moved closer.

"Have you inherited your mummy's special little gift Emily? jeered the voice. Millie realised he sounded different from the man before, he was less wheezy and he spoke with a pronounced lisp instead.

The terrified teenager wriggled against the damp factory wall; hoping against hope that if she pushed hard enough against the slimy brickwork then it would magically give way, open up and take her away from this living hell. Instead she felt the sudden shock of the kidnapper's cold steel blade touch her skin. It started to slowly slice through her underwear; cutting off each of her bra straps. He circled the tip of the knife around the delicate lace that cupped Millie's breasts; tauntingly slipping the metal edge over her shallow cleavage.

"Do you know what's going to happen to you next?" spat the voice, his sinister balaclava'd head tilting from side to side with each sing-song sentence. Millie screamed another muffled cry. She felt every muscle in her body fizz with petrified anticipation, as the blade continued its slow, premeditated journey down towards her lacy panties. She was powerless. Frozen in fear she closed her eyes, resigned to her harrowing fate. She prayed it would be quick, she begged to God it would be painless. She screamed inside believing this would be her last living moment.

Suddenly a heavy iron door in the corner of the building was flung wide open with a loud, jolting bang. Millie's heart raced as she snapped open her eyes to see a dark grey figure standing in the open doorway; a heaven-sent shaft of moonlight flooded through the opening. Was this someone coming to save her?

"What the bloody hell are you doing?" demanded the man, his darkly clothed body silhouetted against the surrounding light. Millie watched him step inside. The man walked with a peculiar gait that was familiar to her. She realised to her dismay it was the asthmatic man who had tormented her the day before. The man with the knife turned briskly towards his accomplice at the doorway, quickly tucking his steel blade into a concealed leather ankle holster.

"Oh we were just getting to know each other," replied the lispy voice, his head twitching nervously from side to side.

"Here, give her this," commanded the now menacing grey figure. He was carrying a large Styrofoam cup that had a straw pushed through the lid. His accomplice ripped away the duct tape and pulled the gag from Millie's mouth before pushing the end of the straw between her lips.

"Dwink this!" he snarled. Millie noticed his speech impediment was more noticeable and he couldn't pronounce his Rs correctly.

"We've got to keep your stwength up for now." The frightened girl compliantly sucked on the plastic tube, grateful that she could at least quench her thirst. The thick liquid clung to her dry throat as she swallowed. Millie thought it tasted vaguely of strawberries but was slightly more powdery and glutinous than a standard milkshake. She was strangely comforted by the idea that giving her a protein drink meant the kidnappers were intending to keep her alive, at least for a while.

"Come on, we've got other work to do tonight," announced the grey figure, as he firmly pushed the oily rag back into Millie's mouth and secured it with new lengths of duct tape.

"Playing with your new toy can wait 'til later," he sneered knowingly at the man with the lisp. Both men walked out through the open doorway into the freedom of the outside world; slamming shut the heavy iron door behind them. Millie heard the sound of a metal chain and the clunk of a padlock slamming shut.

#

Timeline: Monday morning 10am

David Moon had spent the previous night trying to come up with a plan. He knew that his wife's whole empire had been built on a lie. He knew that she would be totally incapable of predicting the lottery numbers correctly. After all, he had helped her to build their psychic domain; he knew full well that the only thing Cellestra Moon could predict with any certain degree of accuracy was tomorrow's date.

When they had first met at the Women's Institute fundraising dinner sixteen years before, David Moon had been immediately impressed by the almost hypnotic ability Carol Frogson possessed; reading people's palms was a well honed party trick that she would use to captivate her audience. When she visited the accountant at his place of work he noticed secretaries in his office always warmed to Carol's bubbly northern personality; they would often ask her for a cheeky tarot reading while she waited in the reception to see him. More often than not David noticed the office workers would be quick to defend Carol's numerous inaccuracies, so long as the majority of what she had said was believable, or what they had wanted to hear.

David soon recognised that Carol possessed a unique skill for understanding people's reactions to whatever she had said. Just like the words written in an open book, she could read the smallest twitch in a willing client's face to betray their inner-most secrets or confirm which guessed detail was correct. Carol could then easily steer the direction of any conversation, encouraging her compliant subjects to reveal more than they realised, and convince them that she really had psychic powers. Cold reading certainly was a lucrative skill that Carol had used to make a modest living out of. But David Moon knew that her 'skill' would only make serious money if it was honed, polished, re-packaged and presented to the world as a 'gift'.

After they had married David became Carol's manager. The scam backstreet psychic was successfully re-branded as the Medium Cellestra Moon. In the early days of the Moon empire, Cellestra's ability for cold reading was embellished with the clever placement of stooges in the crowd and using simple vague statements on stage that would apply to many of the followers in her willing audience. In later years, the advent of technology had enabled the show to use more sophisticated techniques to further manipulate and dupe the Medium's growing fan base.

A few researchers from the production team would pass themselves off as members of the audience. They would strike up seemingly innocent conversations with other people waiting in the foyer before the start of a show and during the interval. These plausible stooges would target a few unwitting victims in the crowd. They would begin the scam by sharing invented hopes and dreams with the innocent marks who had come to see Cellestra's show; sometimes joking that they wondered if great aunt Agatha would come through from the other side and tell them where the money was hidden. Feeling safe in the company of fellow 'believers,' the blissfully unaware victims in the foyer would be completely unguarded. After a couple of gin and tonics they would readily reveal their own secret hopes of receiving a message from a loved one; revealing something known only to them, to put their minds at ease that their dearly departed relatives' spirits were at rest.

The production crew mercilessly absorbed as much information as possible about the unwitting subject's loved ones; times, dates, places and, most importantly, names. The researchers would then spend the remainder of the interval searching online social media sites and ancestry archives for any other valuable specific pieces of information. This would all then be fed to the Medium on stage through a hidden earpiece.

The formula had worked well. With a new name and lots of clever marketing, David Moon had taken a firm grip of the reins and steered Cellestra's career onto TV screens across the land. The television production company had raised phenomenal advertising revenue off the back of the Medium's latest series called 'Cellestra, I Can See You;' a fly-on-the-wall documentary that had followed the Psychic on the road during her sell-out tour of the UK. Cellestra Moon was the kind of cash cow that could not be easily ignored by studio shareholders.

Today, on this bleak Monday morning after the shattering weekend before, David Moon stood and stared blankly at the seven shiny faces before him in the TV studio's main conference room. He had rehearsed his hastily planned presentation over and over during the previous night; this was going to be the pitch of his life and he felt sick. So sick he thought his caffeine-stoked stomach was going to explode. Not only was he scared of how difficult it was going to be to convince these corporate media sharks to go along with his audacious plan, but if ever it leaked out that they had somehow duped the nation with a lottery scam, then the Moons' psychic empire would be finished.

David usually calmed his nerves in these scary situations with a common stress reliever, by imagining the important people he was trying to impress were sitting on the toilet. But today, that tried and tested technique just wasn't working; so he took a little respite by inwardly thinking to himself how the small audience collected in this circular glass-walled office represented every caricature from the television world.

Immediately to his left was an immaculately dressed, slightly camp looking man wearing a navy blue suit and shiny black winkle-picker pointed toe boots. His jacket had been casually opened to reveal a purple silk waistcoat with matching perfectly knotted tie and a very pale pink silk shirt. Even his perfectly styled raven black hair and closely cropped goatee beard had a hint of a purple tint running through them.

'My God', thought David, all he needs are Cellestra's pearls to go with a twin-set like that!

The purple twin-set was in deep and meaningful conversation with a serious looking elderly man who was wearing a blue pinstripe suit and diamond encrusted Rolex watch. David vaguely recognised the older man as being one of the studio's lawyers. An ageing trendy in black jeans, black denim shirt and cream leather cowboy boots sat with his feet nonchalantly balanced on the corner of the conference table while punching in text messages on a wafer thin mobile phone. A mountain of obesity in a brown linen suit filled the space at the opposite end of the conference table. Another man totally lost in a cloud of pungent aftershave tried to look vaguely interested, as a young black man with shiny curly Afro hair sat alongside him, aimlessly flipping through screens on his iPad. A late arrival with artistically messy hair, heavy horn-rimmed glassed and a scruffy hipster rucksack shuffled past the rest of the entourage. He took the remaining empty chair alongside David and proceeded to roll his third joint of the day.

50

"Gentlemen," said David, clearing his throat and standing up to address the group.

"It is of paramount importance that you understand what I am about to tell you can go no further than these four walls." Seven pairs of eyes followed David's every move as he paced across the floor.

"Millie . . . our daughter . . ." he began.

"You mean the one with the perky tits?" came an unexpected jeer from the end of the conference room table. David slowly raised his glance to meet the sweaty round face of the brown suited man who was perched on his chair at the opposite end of the room. The man continued to illustrate his crass jibe by cupping his own man-boobs and giving them a small shake.

'How dare he?' thought David. How dare he even refer to Millie in that way?

"What I was trying to say," continued David, quelling his ruffled annoyance with a cough.

"Cellestra's daughter has been kidnapped," he announced, fighting back a persistent tear. There was a short collective in-take of breath as everyone fixed on what the trembling David Moon was saying.

"The kidnapper has demanded that Cellestra correctly predicts the winning numbers for this weekend's Shimmer Stakes lottery. If she can't predict the numbers then God only knows what'll happen to Millie," said David with a quiver at the end of his voice.

"So what's the problem?" yawned the man wearing the brown suit.

"Is her Cellestraship not up to the challenge?" he added irreverently.

A hushed silence quickly filled every corner of the room. Seven pairs of eyes followed David as he purposefully walked towards the end of the conference table. He could no longer contain his anger at the fat man's jibes; the over-fed studio executive needed to be taught a lesson. Grasping an OHP marker pen off the desk, David straddled the brown suit's swivel chair and quickly raised his left arm to brace across his victim's mountainous chest. David began to scrawl the letters

51

T-I-T in red marking pen across the fat sweaty forehead before him, as six pairs of eyes watched in disbelief.

A slow hand of applause was started off by the man with the smartly trimmed purpley-black goatee beard at the other end of the room. It instantly eased the tension in the room as the rest of the media sheep duly followed. Eventually, stifled giggles erupted into thunderous belly laughs. The purple twin set took a small silver mirror from his waistcoat pocket and passed it down the line to the brown suited man, before standing to take control of the mayhem in the room.

Lynden Brace was a master of his craft; a mentalist who had built a highly lucrative career as a psychological illusionist. This elegant man with a penchant for purple waistcoats and matching ties was an impressive showman with a beguiling repertoire of mind-reading tricks. These were clever illusions which he openly claimed were the results of nothing more than psychological suggestion. His highly entertained audiences were always left in no doubt that his work had nothing to do with spirits, ghosts or ESP. Instead he constantly took great pride in stating that he possessed no psychic gift or ultra-human powers and that his successful stage tricks were a result of body language, mind manipulation and pure showmanship. This fascinating performer's shows didn't attract the hoards of disenchanted people searching for connections with lost souls; instead Lynden Brace's sell-out performances were filled with a strong following of intelligent, open-minded thinkers who had dismissed the paranormal but were fascinated by this hypnotic master of mind control.

Since his first TV appearance at the tender age of twenty-two, Lynden Brace's elaborate and sometimes highly controversial parlour tricks had bewitched audiences throughout the country. The popularity of his 'Brace Yourself' TV series was underpinned by a successful series of tours, CDs, DVDs and books; a veritable library of psychology that had actively encouraged many to hone their own mental abilities.

Now, in the hot goldfish bowl of the television studio's main conference room stood the man, Lynden Brace; in front of this ruffled collection of TV executives, directors and producers he looked like a maestro about to conduct his clueless orchestra.

He had their full and unwavering attention. Slowly, one by one, it dawned on this gaggle of over-paid media monkeys that their hugely expensive bubbles were about to burst; Cellestra Moon, the TV studios' highest paid female star, was in danger of being exposed as a con-artist. Their revenue-spinning flagship series 'I Can See You' would be consigned to the history books as a cruel deception that had taken advantage of hundreds of innocent people when at their lowest ebb. If Cellestra was unmasked as a fraud then their cash cow would be publicly and unceremoniously sent to the knackers' yard.

The only possible way the TV studios could salvage the situation was to make the kidnapper believe that Cellestra Moon had correctly predicted the numbers for the following weekend's lottery. David Moon knew the only man who could successfully create such a masterful illusion, and more importantly help the TV studio to get away with it, was Lynden Brace.

#

Timeline: Monday morning 11am

"Take at look at this, sir," beckoned Sergeant Duke to Richens. Duke had taken a break from scrutinising hours of dull grainy CCTV images taken at the studios and was now following up another, more rewarding line of enquiry. A simple internet search of Cellestra Moon's name had returned thousands of links, but when Duke had filtered the results using an advanced search with other keywords, he had discovered hundreds of websites and social networking pages where the Medium's reputation and credibility were constantly drawn into question. Someone with the username 'MagicMan' had been a regular contributor to many of these forums.

"Looks like we've found ourselves a real internet troll on a mission here," said Duke.

"A troll?" questioned Richens, as he walked over to look at Duke's screen.

"Yes sir, a troll sir." Richens looked at him blankly shaking his head as if to question why the phrase would be familiar to him.

"It's someone who likes to post inflammatory or offensive messages on things like online discussion forums, in chat rooms, social media or on blogs sir."

"And why would they do that Duchess?" asked Richens, still none-the-wiser.

"Well they get a kick out of triggering an emotional response or causing disruption," explained Duke flatly to his techno phobic boss. DS Duke clicked the screen of his laptop.

"On this fan site chat room here for example, you can see a long list of loyal followers posting comments to say how much they had enjoyed one of Cellestra's live shows. Then MagicMan rocks up half way down the page and throws in a message suggesting she's a fraud," continued Duke.

"Yes, but just because he's a sceptic it doesn't make him the kidnapper," said Richens dismissively.

"I know," he agreed.

"But MagicMan's the only Cellestra-basher I've found so far who has actually done time for trolling," said Duke triumphantly.

"He was put away for it. According to our intelligence, and not many people know this, his real name is Kyle Cedel," he continued, handing Richens a case file.

Kyle Cedel had a long cold history of trolling attacks on the internet. His favourite hobby was to invade memorial pages that had been set up in tribute to the dead; posting vile messages that were specifically designed to cause maximum distress to grieving friends and relatives. Initially the internet bully had cowardly hidden behind his first invented persona of 'StarBoy'; launching his attacks from the anonymous sanctuary of his bedroom.

A spindly figure with bad teeth and lank ginger hair, Kyle Cedel had always been an easy target for bullies in the real world; but there, from the sanctuary of his single bed, this keyboard warrior had created a whole new persona; to become the master of his 'virtual' domain with a devoted legion of followers. He could cruelly serve the kind of bullying blows that he had been forced to endure for most of his life. As StarBoy's popularity and notoriety had grown, this nasty internet troll had relished the feeling of power that his new-found status had given him; the escalating obscenity and cruelty of his comments was simply matched by the numbers of people flocking to follow him on their social networking sites. The infamous StarBoy had delighted in his new found adulation, until one day his luck ran dry.

He had mercilessly swooped on a website set up by a bereaved single mother who had lost her baby boy to cot death. Among the loving messages of condolence Cedel's alter ego had cruelly commented:

'You're only upset because it means you'll lose your council house and benefits. Get over it Slut.'

His initial outburst had provoked hundreds to retaliate on line before the grieving mother had a chance to remove his cruel comments from the site. The flurry of rage had soon died down and the website's blog resumed its usual rally of condolence and support for the single mum. Being erased so unceremoniously had angered Kyle Cedel; the perceived lack of respect for his comments prompted StarBoy to fire out his most vile tirade that would lead to his swift arrest.

'You single mothers make me sick. So what, your kid's probably better off dead. What kind of life would it have had anyway? You single sluts just can't keep your legs closed for more than five minutes, so it won't be long 'til you're dropping out another screaming bastard to launch you back to the top of the housing queue again. I know where you live so watch out, 'cos I'll come over and be a spunk donor to help you speed up the process if you like. You could do with a bit of help broadening your gene pool. LOL.' The nasty taunts were littered with laughing emoticons.

Cedel had unwittingly chosen his prey carelessly; he had wrongly assumed that the young mother would not be able to trace him, after all none of his dozens of previous targets had ever found him. His past victims had simply removed his comments from their threads and blocked him from their sites. He had not counted on his latest target being a computer analyst who used to work for the Forensic Science Service. As his vile tirade of comments had spiralled out of control, the net had closed tightly around Kyle Cedel. He had over-stepped the line and the heartbroken grieving mother with a dedicated team of police officers behind her had successfully hunted him down. They tracked his IP address to the dull bedroom he shared with his collection of sci-fi books and fantasy film memorabilia. Kyle Cedel was one of the first to be prosecuted under new anti-cyber abuse laws and was promptly given six months in jail for his thinly veiled threat of sexual assault.

"That's a pretty stiff sentence for being an immature arsehole," said Richens, intrigued by the whole new world of cyber crime that had opened up before him.

"Bet you're not laughing out loud now, eh Cedel?" snorted Duke.

Following his release from prison, Kyle Cedel had quietly resumed his favourite hobby, but now under a new identity, MagicMan. No longer was he the StarBoy who preyed on the vulnerable and grief-stricken; his new focus of attention was the people to whom many had turned for comfort and solace in their bereavement; the psychics, the mediums, the clairvoyants. One of which was Cellestra Moon.

Quick to learn from the careless mistakes he had made as StarBoy, he knew the authorities would be watching him. From that day forward Kyle Cedel would ensure that MagicMan's internet rants would be deemed too insignificant to be considered a direct threat. He would fly just under the radar and would never again be caught out giving a direct written threat. Instead his new, more subtle barrage of attack would be purely hypothetical and based on supposition.

When attacking a psychic's forum he would regularly use his favourite signature statement of 'I believe she hears voices from the other side alright . . . the other side of the auditorium, LOL,' to simply plant the seed of doubt about a celebrity psychic's abilities online. He could then just sit back and watch it bloom into a full on-line attack, as other hungry trolls joined the debate to fan the flames of hatred.

DI Richens eyes flicked through a collection of other documents that were open on DS Duke's screen; a dossier of other people who had all had public disagreements with

Cellestra Moon in the past. Clicking from one to another he suddenly stopped when he reached one that contained a scanned newspaper cutting with an article that questioned how genuine the celebrity Psychic's abilities were.

"I'm not sure about your troll Duchess, but I'd like to see if we can have a chat with the reporter who wrote this article here . . . errr Rosie Carmichael," he said, before forwarding a copy of the document to his own laptop.

#

Since her captors had left the day before, Millie had seen no one. Her dark solitude had only been interrupted by the returning family of rats, who had taken up residence on the mezzanine balcony above her head, along with a solitary sparrow who occasionally flew in and out through the hole in the corrugated iron roof. Millie had taken a little consolation from the long absence of her captors and for the moment, at least, she was alone in her humiliation and despair. The mid morning sun glinted through the hole in the roof, casting its spotlight over the greasy factory floor. Suddenly, out of the corner of Millie's eye, something caught her attention. About half a metre away from her feet, buried within the thick layer of grime, she was sure she could make out the intermittent sparkle of a narrow piece of metal. Was it a knife? Was it a blade? Was it her key to escaping from this captivity?

Slowly she shuffled her legs to one side, taking care not to pull on the twine tethering her to the wall. Placing the palms of her hands flat on the floor behind her, she gradually sank her fingers into the grime, straightening them quickly to raise herself up off the floor. But trying to get up was hopeless, as she was unable to bend her knees; her legs remained bound to the wooden pole that acted like a splint. But deep down Millie knew that if only she could get a little higher up towards the tethering hook above her head, she would be able to get a short distance away from the wall. Surely then she would be able to reach the shiny piece of metal with her out-stretched feet. Millie moved her body up a couple of inches to slacken the twine tied to the rope around her neck.

Slipping back and forth on the black greasy floor she hesitantly edged her way upwards until the full weight of her torso was resting on the tips of her fingers. Her arms began to weaken but she wasn't about to give up now. Blindly she slid her feet over the area where the piece of metal had lain. Where was it? Why couldn't she feel it? Had she imagined it?

Every muscle in her body burned as her heels dragged on the floor; a sharp cramping pain began to stiffen her toes. Her taught forearms trembled but still she would not give up. The twine began to tighten with each attempt like a violin string painfully pulling the burning rope into her neck.

'Just a little further' she thought. 'Just a little further. It must be here somewhere.'

With one deep breath she summoned every ounce of strength from within her, searching her very soul for that extra surge of energy to push herself just another half an inch, but it was no use, she had lost sight of the precious piece of metal in the semi-darkness.

#

Timeline: Monday evening 6pm

A light shower of rain had begun to clear, as the early evening sun broke through the clouds. Rainwater had collected on the uneven grey stone steps leading up to Hanford police station, and the colourful reflection of a distant rainbow danced in its metal framed windows. Breathlessly Rosie Carmichael ran as fast as her navy blue stiletto heels would allow, carefully avoiding the puddles and cracks in the pavement, until finally she arrived at the entrance door.

An angry, overweight mother was escorting a couple of untidy teenagers in hooded tops and baggy pulled-down jeans out through the reception area. The woman slammed the glass door open, ejected her offspring and then squeezed her bulk through the doorframe, forcing Rosie sideways into a brick wall. A strong stench of fried onions clung to the fat woman's bursting pink tracksuit as she slapped each of her sons hard across the back of the head. Screaming a string of obscenities as

58

her wobbly arms pushed the boys into the back seat of a waiting rusty car. The whole circus act then sped off with squealing tyres, drowned out only by the thudding blast of rap music on the car stereo.

'Bloody chavs', shuddered Rosie to herself as she brushed red brick dust from her jacket sleeve and shook a little more grit from her elegantly bobbed chestnut hair. Annoyed by the encounter Rosie regained her composure and made her way through the glass door towards the clerk sitting behind the reception desk.

Rosie Carmichael was a junior reporter for 'The Village', a local weekly newspaper that was delivered free to the houses in the town and given away in petrol stations and grocers' shops. Despite her humble position, Rosie had always regarded her career in journalism as more than a job. For her it was a vocation, a calling, and one day she was sure she would get her big break back into the big time again.

She thought today would be her lucky day. Rosie had been invited to the station by Detective Inspector Richens to see if she could help him with a new investigation. The officer had not given her too many details on the telephone, but Rosie believed the chance of scooping an exclusive story straight from the horse's mouth was too great an opportunity to miss.

Five years previously one of her stories about an alleged 'scam' celebrity Medium had been picked up by the national press. For a short while Rosie had enjoyed a short-lived moment in the spotlight as the reporter to have first broken the exclusive story. But her fifteen minutes of fame had been brought to an abrupt end by the clairvoyant's legal team and the heavy weight of the star's supportive TV production company. Rosie Carmichael's 'scoop' was dismissed as a lie and a total fabrication; the young reporter's burgeoning reputation lay in tatters. The seasoned celebrity Medium, Cellestra Moon, weathered the media storm and continued to forge ahead with her apparently unstoppable success; while an unceremoniously sacked Rosie was left battered and bruised trying to rebuild her fledgling career, with a very long climb back up the media ladder ahead of her.

A uniformed reception clerk lazily picked up the telephone to tell DI Richens his visitor had arrived. She nodded her head towards a couple of black plastic chairs to indicate where Rosie should wait. The young reporter smiled back at the clerk and dutifully took her seat by the window. 'Multi-tasking not in your skill set then?' thought Rosie as she observed the clerk's apparent inability to smile back at her whilst talking on the phone and nodding.

"Thanks for coming in Miss Carmichael." DS Duke was standing in the open doorway to the reception area. Nonchalantly leaning on the doorframe, he beckoned Rosie to follow him into the concrete corridor.

The soulless tunnel was a dank grey artery that fed people and information to the police station's nerve centre. Rosie followed closely behind DS Duke's long strides as he led her past numerous offices, interview rooms and waiting areas that were busy with the sounds of trilling telephones and raised voices. They took a lift to the first floor and finally arrived at a door that led into the CID office

Detective Inspector Richens was sat behind his grey metal desk, closely reading a couple of sheets of newspaper set in front of him. Rosie had worked in printing rooms from when she was a teenager on work experience; so the ability to read documents upside-down was second nature to the journalist. Rosie felt a little uneasy as she could clearly read the headlines and make out her own name printed beneath as the author of the articles.

"Come in Miss Carmichael," invited Richens, his gaze remaining firmly fixed on the paperwork in front of him.

"Please take a seat while my Sergeant goes to get us some coffees," he smiled presumptively as DS Duke left the room.

Rosie quietly sat down on a grey plastic seat opposite Richens; her inquisitive green eyes flashing around the dull, sparsely furnished space. The area had been temporarily assigned as a CID office while the decorators were in giving the rest of the building its annual lick of pale grey paint. A quarter of the very large room had been cordoned off with padded blue acoustic screens to create a temporary dividing wall. This gave the sergeant and his senior colleague a workspace that was separated from the chaos of the main office. The other side of the room was assigned to a team of detectives and administrative staff.

In the Inspector's area an empty cork notice board hung loosely on the wall above a large modern metal desk with rounded edges; a matching grey metal waste bin tucked underneath. On top of the desk was a very old, small cubic television with a built-in DVD player. In a futile attempt to make their domain feel less utilitarian, Duke had brought in an un-loved plump green spider plant from home and draped it across the top of a gunmetal grey filing cabinet in the opposite corner of the space. Rosie couldn't help thinking that the plant was in desperate need of a drink of water. A little further along the wall was a free-standing white melamine incident board that Rosie noticed had been freshly wiped clean.

Through a space in the temporary dividing wall, Rosie could see a flat screen TV was hung on the far wall in the detectives' area; its sound had been muted but the young reporter could still see the rolling news stories of the day flicker across the bottom of the screen. The sounds of distant sirens, buzzing telephones, bleeping pagers and police officers scuttling up and down the corridor outside filled the air. Rosie could hear three or four CID officers speaking in hushed tones as they sat at a row of temporary desks behind the blue padded acoustic screen. Everything was beginning to merge into a low hum of irritating background noise, as Rosie patiently waited for DI Richens to speak.

An uneasy silence cloaked the area by Richens' desk, as he continued his close inspection of the newspaper articles in front of him. Eventually, after several minutes, he slowly raised his head to look at Rosie; a watery smile began to grow beneath his thin pointed nose.

"It caused quite a sensation didn't it," said Richens, at last the dull silence had ended. Rosie looked at him quizzically, still unsure why she had been summoned to the police station.

"I mean your attempt to unmask the country's most adored Medium," he added as he deftly spun the newspaper cuttings around to face the young woman.

"Yes, it did at the time," replied Rosie feeling protective towards her articles.

"I bet you feel quite resentful towards Cellestra Moon now don't you?" said Richens with a slightly accusing manner.

"She almost ruined your career didn't she Miss Carmichael?"

Rosie felt an unexpected stab of anger rise up through her body, as the memories of the humiliation she had felt came flooding back; the way the media had been so quick to turn the tables on the fledgling reporter, accusing her of attempting to ruin the TV personality's career. The libel case was taken to court, as Cellestra Moon's lawyers claimed that Rosie's short series of articles were totally unfounded.

Rosie remembered how she had picked up the story about a scam Psychic from a local radio station. The late-night phone-in talk show had broadcast a call from someone called Casey. He said he had been working as a lighting engineer at a Cellestra Moon show and had heard someone at the back of the auditorium feeding the Medium on stage with information about people in the audience. A few other listeners had also called in to the radio show to say they'd been at the same event and had heard it too. Rosie had then used her contacts at the radio station to successfully track down a telephone number for Casey. He had been most obliging during their lengthy conversations, giving Rosie all the slanderous ammunition she needed to write her thought provoking articles. He told her how he had seen people from Cellestra's production team chatting to audience members in the foyer beforehand, to gain the valuable information needed to feed to the Medium on stage through a hidden earpiece. Unknown to the innocent junior reporter, her thought provoking column that questioned the morality of celebrity clairvoyants, was about to open Pandora's Box, and Rosie would feel the whole weight of national media break her provincial world apart.

"You naively tried to expose Cellestra Moon as a fraud, but instead you stirred up a hornet's nest that would sting you so hard that you would never be taken seriously as a reporter again," accused Richens.

"No, it wasn't like that," protested Rosie.

"When Casey told me what he had witnessed I ran the story in good faith. I gave the TV company lots of opportunities to respond but they didn't return any of my calls. How the hell was I supposed to know that Cellestra Moon was being primed as the next big thing to hit our screens? Of course the studio wouldn't want all of the time, effort and money they had ploughed into the fat old cow's new show to go down the pan would they? So they had to defend her to the hilt." Rosie sat back in her seat, momentarily pleased with her robust answer.

"They did a damn good job defending her though didn't they?" retorted Richens.

"Let me see now . . ." he shuffled through a ring-bound collection of neatly typed A4 sheets of paper.

"Ah yes, your employers had to pay some hefty damages at the end of the court case didn't they Rosie," he prodded, hoping for a reaction. Rosie stared down at the grey painted concrete floor, her pale face framed by her bob of chestnut brown hair; her green eyes began to fill with shallow tears. She realised that today was not going to be her lucky day after all, as she was forced to cast her mind back to the darkest episode of her life.

"Excuse me sir," mumbled DS Duke as he entered the room. He was awkwardly carrying a cup of coffee in each hand, with a couple of manila folders tucked under one arm. A small white square envelope was precariously wedged beneath his chin and pressed firmly towards his chest. Rosie looked up from staring at the floor; she arose slightly from her hard plastic seat and reached out to relieve some of Duke's burden by taking one of the steaming plastic cups.

"Well?" continued Richens, trying to ignore the unwelcome interruption from his sergeant.

"You cost your employers a small fortune in damages didn't you?" He glared at the young woman sat opposite. Rosie repositioned herself on the seat and turned the coffee cup between her fingers.

"Yes, we lost the case; yes, I lost my job. I suppose when it came to manipulating the national press the TV company simply had more clout than I did," she lamented.

"When the shit hit the fan Casey was nowhere to be found. Like a prize fool I'd always respected his anonymity. I'd never actually met him face-to-face, but we'd spoken at length on the phone. His number was a pay-as-you-go mobile. I tracked down his address but it was a run-down bed and breakfast and they didn't keep accurate records of the people who stayed there," she whined.

"Come to think of it, the only trace of Casey ever having been at the B&B was a couple of sci-fi books and a few fantasy film posters that he'd left behind. He was obviously some sad little prick with a grudge. Dragging me into his attack on that stupid fat cow ruined my life."

Duke put down the other coffee cup in front of DI Richens and let the folders and square white envelope slide from his grip and cascade onto the desk. The awkward silence returned to the room as Richens looked quizzically at Rosie. She had begun to stare blankly at the desk in front of her as if deep in thought. She paused for breath and took a sip of coffee; the surprisingly hot liquid scalded her top lip. In an effort to regain her composure, she pushed back a persistently annoying lock of shiny chestnut hair back behind her ear before continuing to answer Richen's question.

"So, the TV studios managed to convince anyone who cared to listen that my story was a lie; that my 'source' was at best an unreliable nutter or at worst a figment of my creative imagination. They claimed in the end that Casey didn't exist and I had fabricated the whole article." Dewy tears began to well in Rosie's eyes.

Richens took a sip of his hot coffee and couldn't help a small feeling of compassion for the young woman. He began to think how this once feisty go-getter had probably resigned herself to the fact that she would never rise above her current pay grade. No matter how competent a reporter she was or how hard she tried, the scandal would always be there; haunting her, waiting to push her back down into the gutter at the first opportunity. She was a potential liability and no large newspaper would be willing to take the risk of employing her, so the best position she could ever aspire to would be a junior role on a local rag.

"Look Inspector, I came here today because my Editor said I might be able to help you with a line of enquiry, but if you've just got me out here today to talk about an old shit story that I ran years ago then I've told you all I know; I really don't know how I can help you any more," said Rosie impatiently as she shuffled in her seat. Richens continued to read the paperwork on his desk.

"I was naive and stupid at the time, I admit it. I didn't do my research properly and I paid the price," continued Rosie. She was beginning to feel extremely anxious and very annoyed that there was no exclusive scoop today; just a re-hash of old news. Her green eyes began to twitch uncontrollably and she subconsciously began to scratch an itch on her left forearm. Finally, DI Richens looked up and leaned back in his seat. He rubbed his tired eyes then ran his fingers through his greying hair before bringing his hands to rest behind his head.

"You look a bit different now compared with how you looked back then don't you," said Richens accusingly, as he nodded towards an old head and shoulders shot of Rosie in the newspaper article on his desk. Her face was rounder in the photograph, her mousey brown hair tied up in a tight bun on top of her head.

"I'd say you look like you've lost quite a lot of weight since then Miss Carmichael, a few stone in fact." Rosie stared at the newspaper cuttings on the desk in front of her, wondering where the detective's accusing tone would lead.

"It must have hit you hard Rosie," soothed Richens, his voice slightly softer now. The young reporter remained silent.

"You were once a large fish in a small pond and suddenly, when your story broke, you were catapulted into the big rough ocean. Your fall from grace brought you back to the slimy puddle you came from, and that hit you very hard didn't it?" He paused.

"It hit you so hard in fact you managed to get yourself a nasty little drugs habit into the bargain didn't you?" Richens simultaneously slid two other pieces of paper across the desk in front of Rosie. One was a toxicology report from four years before; the other a record of the young reporter's caution for drugs possession. It was unexpectedly damming evidence that confirmed Rosie Carmichael had nearly taken her own life with a heroin overdose. A shocked Rosie stared silently at the

65

incriminating pieces of paper in front of her; she felt as if her life's blood was draining away from her brain, down her body and out to the tips of her stiletto shoes.

"No!" she shouted. "It wasn't like that. What the hell is this? Character assassination day?" She could feel the anxiety creeping through her body; the memories returning to haunt her; the persistent itch in her arm getting worse.

"How did it happen Rosie?" demanded Richens relentlessly.

"How did what happen?" replied Rosie. She suddenly felt vulnerable and wondered where Richen's line of enquiry was leading.

"Excuse me, but am I being accused of something here?" Rosie shuffled up on her seat.

"No, you're not being accused of anything. I was referring to your little habit," replied Richens, cutting off the young woman's protest.

"Did it start with a little puff of weed Rosie, you know just to get you through the stress of the working day? A snort of bubble to get you going in the morning? A tab of E there? And before you know it, it's turned into a little line of coke for breakfast each day," he carried on.

"Suddenly you're out of your depth; you're hitting the high life and promoting your dirty habit to a syringe of heroin." He stared back at her angrily.

"The shit that you shoved in your veins ruined your career Miss Carmichael; not your convenient mystery man Casey, not the TV company who sued your sorry little arse and certainly not Cellestra Moon." Rosie stared back at Richens, her green eyes filling with plump tears. Why were the police so interested in her connection to Cellestra Moon after all these years?

"This scrawny new slim line look of yours?" goaded Richens relentlessly, reaching across the desk to grab Rosie's left hand.

"What's that then, heroin chic? he spat, as he wrenched the sleeve of Rosie's jacket up her arm to reveal two pale red track lines.

Rosie was speechless. For once in her life she couldn't find the right words to argue her case. She pulled away from Richens, laid her glossy chestnut-bobbed head in her hands and began to cry. Richens opened the square white envelope that had been resting on his desk and removed a couple of print-outs and a CD from inside.

"I can quite understand how upsetting it must be for you to have to re-live the worst chapter in your life so far," continued Richens a little softer, as he loaded the CD into the player. "But there is something I need you to listen to before you leave here today."

#

Cellestra sat at the top of her king size divan in the Moon's bedroom. David had managed to coax his wife to leave the sanctuary of her dressing room at the studio and return to their home in the country for the evening. The doctor had prescribed a sedative to help the fretful woman to sleep but it had not had much effect as Cellestra slowly rocked back and forth on the bed, clutching her purple and gold cashmere shawl tightly to her chest. To Cellestra her life was in suspended animation. There was no yesterday, no tomorrow; just another slowly ticking day that would soon end and bring her another step closer to the time when she had to publicly denounce her psychic abilities to the unsuspecting world. David Moon took his wife in his arms, hugging her closely into his chest.

"Don't worry angel, we'll get her back" he soothed.

"That's just it though," sobbed Cellestra, gazing up hopelessly at her husband.

"I just can't see how we're gonna get out of this without everything coming out in the press; without everyone finding out the truth. We're going to lose everything. The tour, the book deals, the TV show. This house. Everything."

David sat upright and turned his wife towards him, firmly placing a reassuring hand on each shoulder, he gazed into her tear-swollen eyes. He tried to ignore the nagging realisation that Cellestra had made no mention of losing her daughter in the scenario. It wasn't completely lost on him that Cellestra had placed more importance on her career and material possessions than her own daughter's life.

"Cellestra, I have never let you down and I'm not about to start now," he soothed.

"I'm not about to let some bastard take everything we've worked so hard for away from us. You need to trust me Ce and listen carefully to what I have to say. Do you understand?" Cellestra took in a deep breath and nodded.

"I have found a way of giving the kidnapper what he wants," continued David.

"The production company is with me on this and we have the best crew available to help pull it off. All we need is for you to agree and we can set all the wheels in motion."

"What do you mean?" asked Cellestra dejectedly.

"It's not like I've suddenly developed psychic powers is it?" David looked back at his wife and took in a deep breath to quell his annoyance.

"I know that you stupid cow," he spat. Cellestra stared back at her husband quizzically.

"So, I've asked Lynden Brace to stage a one off TV special along the lines of his 'Brace Yourself' stuff, but it will involve the lottery show next weekend," he explained.

"You'll have a sequence of numbers to give to the kidnapper. Brace will then pull off his mind bending jiggery-pokery stuff to make it appear that the same numbers come up in the live draw. We can then cash in the winning ticket. The kidnapper will then have no hold over you. He'll have his ransom money and he'll have to let Millie go. What's more, if the shit hits the fan and the press get wind of the scam, then it'll be Lynden Brace's reputation on the line, not yours."

Cellestra smiled back at her husband and once more felt reassured. She realised this was one of the reasons why she had found it so easy to fall in love with the accountant all those yeas ago; as once more she so readily handed over the reins of her career to the man she trusted without question.

#

Timeline: Monday night

Throughout the evening at Hanford police station Rosie had re-lived and re-counted every moment of Cellestragate; from when she had first heard the radio phone-in show; to her demotion to the bottom of the food chain on a local rag's news desk. Not one detail had been over-looked as each piece of information she had given to Richens and Duke was questioned and scrutinised. She had never actually met Casey face-to-face. This hungry, naive reporter, who blindly ran the mystery man's story, had stupidly only ever spoken to him on the telephone. Now, here in this grey utilitarian building she could hear the same softly spoken almost effeminate voice coming from the CD player; the same slanderous tone that had difficulty pronouncing the letter R; the venomous voice that she believed had been the evil source of her very public and painful downfall.

"I believe she hears voices from the other side alright; the other side of the auditorium."

"That's him. You've got the fucker. That's Casey" shouted Rosie as she excitedly sprang up from her plastic seat.

"Where is he? Just wait 'til I get my hands on that vindictive little bastard," she shouted. DS Duke looked back at Rosie with an awkward smile as DI Richens casually shuffled the manila folders on his desk into a neat pile.

"I'm afraid we don't have him yet Miss Carmichael." The adrenalin began to drain from Rosie's body as quickly as it had rushed through her veins on hearing the voice of her Nemesis. The itching in her arm was getting worse. Richens casually leaned back in his swivel chair.

"This is simply a recording of the original radio show that Casey called in to," said Duke almost apologetically.

"Then why?" asked Rosie, sitting back down again.

"What the hell has all this been about?" she whined, turning away to stare at the grey painted concrete floor again.

"I just needed someone to positively ID the sound of his voice as being the voice of someone with a serious grudge against Cellestra Moon," said Richens, returning his swivel chair to an upward position.

69

Rosie spun around in anger, a wall of fiery rage building from deep inside her; there it was again that horrible woman's name being paraded in front of her. In Rosie's mind the police officers' barrage of pointless repetitive questions had simply raked over the corpse of her career. Now this bristle faced DI had kept taunting her by throwing in the name of the woman who Rosie believed had been at the very source of her downfall. Rosie took a lung expanding deep breath, clenched the fingers tightly in both of her hands and lurched towards Richens, unleashing the full torrent of her pent up anger as she jumped up from her plastic seat.

"What?" screamed Rosie incredulously, punching her right fist past Richens' pointed nose before bringing it back down to land sharply on the metal desk in front of him. DS Duke leaped around from the other side of the office to restrain Rosie from trying to successfully deliver her second blow.

"Come on Rosie, don't be stupid. Hitting a police officer is a serious offence," said Duke, trying to calm the young woman as he grasped her shoulders and pulled her away from the desk. Richens staggered backwards on his swivel chair, trying to regain his composure, as Rosie continued with a verbal assault.

"You mean you got me all the way over here on the pretence of me working with you on a case; to cruelly drag up all that old shit and remind me of all those terrible mistakes I've made. Then you give me a small crumb of hope by making me think you've got the twisted little bastard who ruined my career; when all along you're just more interested in helping out that over-paid fat-arsed freak show?"

As she tried to wriggle free of DS Duke's firm hold, Rosie could feel her face flushing with anger. The itching in her forearm beginning to nag again; the twitching in her green eyes revealed her innermost secret.

"Why the hell would the police give a flying monkey about people with a grudge against Cellestra fucking Moon of all people anyway?" she stared accusingly at Richens, escaping Duke's protective grip.

"I'm sorry Ms Carmichael," replied Richens coldly.

"I can't give you any details of what we are investigating at the moment, but I assure you that as soon as I can tell the press anything, you'll be among the first to know." He smiled as DS Duke led Rosie towards the open doorway. Reluctantly she followed Duke out of the office before straightening her crumpled suit and walking away down the soulless corridor towards the lift.

Richens got up from his swivel chair and picked up a marker pen. He confidently strode over to the free-standing blank white incident board, before flipping the melamine sheet back over to reveal his notes about the kidnapping case. At the centre of the board was a smiling photograph of Millie Moon, along with a short summary of the known circumstances surrounding her abduction.

At the top of the board was a photograph of Millie's abandoned car on the studio car park; at the bottom a couple of photographs of the pile of clothes, Millie's personal effects and the dead body discovered in Witches Wood. At the far left edge of the board the Inspector had started to compile a short list of the names of any people connected with Millie Moon; so far it only had the names of Cellestra and David Moon written beneath. On the right hand side Duke had written any other names that had been mentioned as part of the investigation: Kyle Cedel, StarBoy, MagicMan and the mysterious, softly spoken Casey.

'Bloody stuck-up junkie,' thought Richens as he made a mental note to keep a close watch over Miss Rosie Carmichael; before adding her name to the list on the right hand side of the incident board.

Chapter 6

Timeline: Tuesday morning

Lynden Brace was relaxing in the comfortable embrace of a sumptuous black leather swivel chair; idly gazing out of the window of a television producer's office. He was aimlessly staring at the summer rain drizzling down the glass wall of office windows when his attention was momentarily drawn to a large gangly spider sheltering outside in the corner of a pane of glass. A spider of that size would immediately strike terror into the hearts of numerous secretaries should it be allowed to run freely inside the office; but here it was reduced to clinging on to life beneath a small strip of adhesive tape that had been carelessly left there long ago by a window fitter. Lynden was struck by the realisation that this fearsome creature's world had suddenly become so fragile. Caught eleven floors up battling against the elements, all it could do was hold on and wait for the rain to stop. It was so prophetic thought Lynden, if only the sun would come out, then the spider could spin a dry web to protect itself and catch food. He couldn't help feeling how delicate the balance of life could be sometimes. It was as if one moment life could appear to quite literally hang in the balance with no way of escape; yet with a simple ray of sunshine a life could be totally enriched or in some extreme cases, saved.

The TV executive's office décor was a fantastic shrine to nineties' interior design and Lynden was surprised to see how out-dated it seemed. The room featured a large black ash desk, topped in smoked glass; two black leather swivel chairs on one side and an over-sized recliner on the other. This chair was set intentionally higher than the two opposite, to subliminally exert the TV Producer's self-proclaimed authority, in an effort to either impress or intimidate whoever sat before him. A Cappuccino machine purred seductively in the corner of the room and a bank of fitted cupboards on one wall were set around an over-sized built-in TV screen. This interior homage to the nineties was finished off with a highly impractical thick pile cream carpet that felt like freshly driven snow when walked on.

Brendan Fagg pushed open his office door. Lynden observed the large, slightly dishevelled looking man as he squeezed his bulky frame through the opening. He noticed the sweaty faced TV Producer was wearing the same brown cotton suit that he had worn at the meeting in the boardroom with David Moon the day before. Lynden smiled inwardly as he deduced that either it was the same outfit, or Brendan Fagg could only find suits in one style and colour in his size.

"Mister Brace, thank you so much for coming in to see me today," said Brendan warmly, as he heartily shook Lynden's extended hand, before taking his place behind the desk on the over-sized chair.

"Think nothing of it," Lynden responded graciously whilst savouring the fact that the heavy-weight TV Producer had reverently called him Mister Brace.

". . . and please, do call me Lynden," he added whilst gazing at Brendan's forehead to check for any signs of David Moon's marking pen.

"Thank you Lynden," smiled Brendan, feeling slightly less awkward. The portly TV Producer shuffled a few papers on his desk and cleared his throat before starting his over-rehearsed speech.

"You see, the thing is . . . following our meeting yesterday you know we need to create the illusion that Cellulite Moo can accurately predict the lottery. In fact the whole empire built around her reputation relies on it." Lynden smiled inwardly again. He was beginning to relish in the fact that the TV Producer was faltering by unnecessarily recapping previous facts; a classic sign of nervousness or playing for time. He also picked up on the lack of respect that Brendan Fagg had for his hottest TV star by his unexpected mention of Cellestra's studio nickname. Lynden nodded reassuringly and purposefully locked Brendan Fagg in his line of sight.

"Well, the thing is Mister Brace . . . err . . . I mean Lynden. You're our only hope. I mean don't get me wrong, I haven't forgotten the debacle when that twatty Dave Moon scrawled on my face with a marker pen yesterday." Lynden's hawk-like gaze remained firmly locked on to Brendan Fagg's eyes as the comical memory of the impromptu skin graffiti flooded through his mind.

"Something like that wouldn't normally be tolerated, but I had to give him the chance to let off a bit of steam, I mean I was a bit disrespectful about his kid at first. But I speak as I find and I did only say what everyone else was thinking about her tits," he added defensively. Lynden watched the sweating bulk of brown cotton shift uneasily in his swivel armchair.

'Why, I do believe mister big and powerful TV Producer is feeling rather vulnerable?' thought Lynden, still secretly laughing inside at the Cellulite Moo nickname. Brendan carried on delivering his speech, occasionally dabbing a folded silk handkerchief across his forehead and top lip.

"The truth is Lynden, between you and me, I need to keep David Moon and his over-stuffed wife firmly on board, or my bonuses for the next ten years will be floating up the swan's arse," continued Brendan. Lynden noticed another heavy bead of sweat forming across the TV Executive's quivering top lip.

"We haven't a clue at the studio how to pull it off, and I was wondering if you'd got any ideas yet?" The heavyweight studio executive slumped back in his recliner and tried to stifle his deep sigh. The awful humiliation of having to beg someone for help was over. His speech had been delivered. All Brendan had to do now was to listen to Lynden's ideas and negotiate the fee.

Lynden remained relaxed in his swivel chair, bathing in the heavy aroma of the newly sewn leather and the feel of the thick cream Axminster carpet beneath his feet. Slowly, as if deep in thought, he took in a purposeful breath and ran the fingers of his right hand through the purple-black hairs of his smartly clipped goatee beard. As if pondering the whole world's problems, Lynden closed his eyes momentarily and then tilted his head back to stare at the ceiling. Slowly he lowered his gaze and looked back thoughtfully at the sweating TV Producer.

"Well?" nudged Brendan impatiently.

"Yes," said Lynden. "I think I can help you."

Before Lynden could utter another word Brendan Fagg had risen to his feet. He trudged through the pile of thick cream carpet and made his way to Lynden's side of the desk to heartily thank him with a crushing man-hug.

"But," said Lynden; escaping from the overwhelming clutch of brown cotton.

"It has to be totally on my terms," he added. Lynden's heart danced inside as he secretly relished in the situation of being the only man able to help.

Lynden Brace had no genuine desire to help Cellestra Moon, and he would not be creating this illusion as a favour to a fellow entertainer. Instead he regarded the whole event as a professional challenge and seized the opportunity to negotiate a lucrative contract with the country's top TV studio. He had them at his mercy. Now he was going to make them pay.

When Lynden had started his career, television companies were not interested in his style of entertainment. They had all dismissed his ideas for a show as either small time tricks akin to street scams or fairground hustles; his more elaborate illusions were wrongly deemed to be too long-winded for the short attention span of an average television audience. It was only by initially making radical changes to his show that he convinced the first cable station to run a small pilot series. Following the first transmission his reputation quickly grew. His social media videos regularly went viral and within a few years he had managed to build a highly revered reputation as a first class mentalist. Now the biggest television studio in the land was knocking on his door. They needed his help and he was going to make them pay handsomely for their earlier ignorance of his incomparable talent.

Brendan Fagg returned to his over-sized recliner and sat in silence, slowly absorbing all of Lynden's measured demands. At the end of a very long cappuccino-fuelled two-hour meeting Lynden and Brendan were shaking hands and ready to sign an agreement.

"Finally though," said Lynden, rising elegantly from his chair.

"My lawyers will insist that my part in fooling the nation by fixing the lottery draw is on record as being under protest, and that I have only agreed to take part to help secure the safe return of Cellestra Moon's kidnapped daughter."

Lynden knew this whole illusion would be seriously fraudulent. If it worked, then anyone who had bought a Shimmer Stakes lottery ticket for that weekend's draw would have been conned. The repercussions could be catastrophic; there would be a national outcry if anyone ever discovered the truth. It would throw the whole integrity of the lottery game into utter turmoil and could potentially end Lynden Brace's career.

"In the event of anyone ever finding out that the show was an illusion, then I want it to be on the record that I worked with the full knowledge and co-operation of the TV production company, and on the orders of the police," concluded Lynden. Brendan nodded in reluctant agreement. He knew he was beaten. His company not only had to protect their highest paid psychic star but they also needed to maintain their lucrative contract with Shimmer Stakes to host its lottery draw show.

"Okay," said Brendan with a watery smile.

"I'll tell David Moon that they can send the kidnapper his text. Cellestra Moon will accurately predict the following Saturday's lottery draw numbers."

"Excellent," replied Lynden with a slightly camp celebratory clap of his hands.

"Can I just borrow your tablet for a moment Brendan to log on to my social networking accounts? I might as well get the viral wheels in motion straight away," he asked, presumptively flipping open the screen on the executive's desk.

#

Timeline: Tuesday evening

Rosie Carmichael had spent the whole of the last twenty-four hours scanning the internet for any mention of the pseudonym MagicMan. That had been one of the two upside-down names she had seen written on the manila folders that had fallen from DS Duke's arms onto Richens' desk. She assumed they were pertinent to an investigation as they had been circled in red. Also it was more than likely they were associated with Cellestra Moon, as that had been the police officer's only topic of conversation when questioning her. The young reporter had

76

sat on the sofa in her living room with a laptop computer; working methodically throughout the night and day; relentlessly scouring the web, hunting down her Nemesis. Cross matches with the name Casey had given no results of any significance, just old court reports from her libel case. But when she had searched for Cellestra Moon along with the name she had seen written on one of Duke's folders, she had discovered a whole plethora of old forums and chat rooms where MagicMan had lain dormant for a few months. Was he patiently waiting to pounce again?

Excited by the results of her new line of enquiry, Rosie leapt up from the sofa and went into the kitchen. She opened the fridge door and took out a bottle of chilled Rosé wine. She smiled as she returned to the living room to pour some more wine into her glass. At last she believed she had found a breakthrough, and it was going to be another long night.

Hours passed by as the young reporter frantically tapped the keys on her laptop. More searches, more cross-matching; but there were still no more clues to confirm any connection between the mysterious Casey and MagicMan.

"Damn," she cursed. MagicMan hadn't commented about Cellestra Moon anywhere for months.

Rosie's vacant expression and deliberate long pauses during her meeting in Richen's office had given her an opportunity to scrutinise some of the paperwork on the Inspector's desk. Burying her head in her hands and pretending to cry had drawn her gaze closer to the manila envelopes.

"If only I'd have been able to read the name on the second folder; that may have given me a better chance of a cross-match." Rosie took another sip of wine.

"Where the hell are you? You bastard," she muttered before suddenly spotting his name on another clairvoyant's open forum page. Blinking back at her from the rows of text she clearly found the connection she had been searching for. MagicMan's tag next to a short comment:

'I believe she hears voices from the other side alright, the other side of the auditorium.'

"He's at it again," she squealed. Rosie gasped a sudden intake of air as a shudder flew down her spine. It was too much of a coincidence to be anyone other than the elusive Casey. She realised MagicMan and Casey were the same person. The reporter's mind began to flip through anything else she could remember from her numerous conversations with the man on the phone five years ago. It was difficult, as most of the reporter's drug-fuelled memories of that time in her life were generally quite hazy. Suddenly she felt a stinging burst of excitement shoot through her chest as she remembered what she'd told DI Richens had been found in Casey's abandoned room at the bed and breakfast.

". . . a couple of sci-fi books and a few fantasy film posters that he'd left behind . . . YES!" shouted Rosie, raising a fist into the air. "That's where he'll be."

Rosie trawled through a seemingly endless list of sci-fi forums, relentlessly searching for any sign of her Nemesis. After four long hours she was about to give up on her new line of investigation before something caught her eye on a fantasy film appreciation site. MagicMan's username was listed as a regular visitor to its chat room.

"It's got to be him," she rasped excitedly, gulping down another glass of wine.

"MagicMan is definitely Casey."

Hesitantly Rosie clicked open a window on the site to register as a fan. That was the only way she would be able to gain access to the chat rooms and strike up a conversation with MagicMan. Behind the guise of her newly invented persona called Magician's Assistant, Rosie nervously typed in a brief description for her online profile and quickly pressed the send button. Almost immediately her mobile phone beeped into action to indicate she had a text message. Quickly Rosie opened up her inbox. Her heart raced as she used the authorisation code in the message to access the fan site's chat room. She was in.

Boldly, she left a small introductory note on MagicMan's message board, requesting a hook up.

Chapter 7

Timeline: Wednesday afternoon

DS Duke was struggling to keep his heavy tired eyes open, as he continued to scan the countless hours of additional CCTV recordings that had been sent to him from the television studios. Almost hypnotised by the monotonous grainy flickering on the screen, he had watched a stampede of stiletto heels and briefcases rush through the building at the start and end of each day. In between, there had been a steady flow of people all caught on camera. Personal assistants and crew members ran along the corridors; fast food deliveries arrived; motorcycle couriers with important packages came and went, as well-known personalities drifted through on their way from dressing rooms to stage sets. Everyone had been accounted for and Duke was getting restless. He had watched hours of activity and yet there was still no sign of anything out of the ordinary; no glimpse of anyone who shouldn't have been there.

"Right, let's take a look at this one from the foyer," sighed Duke as he loaded another DVD into the player.

Richens looked across at his Sergeant momentarily. The Inspector was relaxing at his desk with an overdue syrupy black coffee and the Times' crossword. Deep in thought he returned his gaze to his newspaper and began tapping his pen on the edge of the metal desk; much to the annoyance of his colleague.

"Could you stop doing that please, sir," asked Duke.

"It's very distracting."

The tapping ceased immediately. Richens looked up and noisily shuffled his newspaper, folding it open at the brain-teaser page and then folding it down to a more manageable size so he could easily return to finish the crossword later. Duke looked across and tutted.

"What's the matter Duchess? Can't you cope with a little background noise?" he chided.

"It's not that I can't cope sir, it's just very annoying to have a constant tapping, clicking and shuffling going on when I'm trying to concentrate on the . . ." he broke off his conversation when something on the screen caught his eye. Richens sensed the sudden surprise in his sergeant's voice. He got up and stepped over to Duke's desk to take a closer look.

It was a CCTV recording of Cellestra's autograph signing in the foyer. The image from the foyer was of better quality than the seemingly endless loop of grainy grey films from the rest of the TV studios. It was slightly higher resolution and in full colour. Both men watched the short ten seconds of film as it was re-wound and re-played for the fourth time. An elegant woman with curly red hair, wearing large rose tinted sunglasses approached a crowd of adoring fans. In the woman's hand was a lavender coloured oblong package that she passed to Cellestra Moon.

"Zoom in, zoom in for God's sake man," shouted Richens in frustration. On hearing the inspector's agitated tone, a group of detectives began to make their way over from the main office and quickly gathered around Duke's desk.

"Damn it, most of the people in the crowd are wearing those bloody stupid rose tinted sunglasses. How are we ever gonna get an ID from that?" Richens clapped his hands together to summon everyone's attention. He perched on the edge of Duke's desk to address his small team of officers.

"Right, Duchess here has had a breakthrough," he announced. Duke winced at the use of his nickname.

"He's found the bit of CCTV with what looks like a woman handing over the ransom phone," added Richens. A small spluttering of applause flowed around the room.

"I want her every move in that building tracked; where she came from, where she went. She's wearing a disguise at the point of contact but we must have her on some other footage from the building without those stupid glasses on. I want all of you to muck in and watch every last second of CCTV. No-one leaves tonight until we find her."

"Excuse me DI Richens," enquired a small voice from a petite fair-haired woman standing in the doorway. Richens turned swiftly towards her, enraged that anyone should interrupt him in mid-flow of issuing orders to his CID team.

"What?" he barked. ". . . and who the hell are you?" The young blonde nervously entered as the room fell silent.

"I'm DC Trudi Jones sir; I work in the new Cyber Unit."

The mere mention of there being such a thing as a Cyber Unit sent a stifled murmur of laughter flowing through the room; as various officers started to emulate robotic movements and recite 'exterminate, exterminate!' in hushed robotic voices.

"DS Duke asked us to track down the IP addresses for anyone who has been involved in posting messages about Cellestragate," Trudi began, her voice starting to tremble nervously.

"I . . . err I hope you don't mind me interrupting . . . but I think I've found the identity of the main internet troll sir," she smiled. Richens raised his eyebrows and stood up from where he had been perched on the corner of Duke's desk. With one glance from their boss the whole of the department fell silent once more.

"The person calling themselves MagicMan was all over social networking sites and religious forums until a few months ago, ranting on about how the likes of Cellestra Moon are con artists and charlatans," continued Trudi.

"He's gone a bit quiet recently but he's still got quite a hefty web footprint, and I've tracked down his IP to someone called Kyle Cedel . . . here's his address," Trudi took in a triumphant deep breath as she handed DI Richens a memo sheet.

"Cedel has got form for . . ."

"Yes I know," interrupted Richens coldly.

"I was privy to his confidential file," he added, in a slightly dismissive attempt to exert his authority over the junior officer.

"He's done time for trolling in the past when he was once called StarBoy," Richens proudly announced, trying to impress his team with the fact that he was familiar with the term 'internet troll' and knew all about Kyle Cedel's sordid little pastime.

"But that still doesn't make him a kidnapper Jones . . . unless . . ." Richens trailed off his sentence as if entering another one

81

of his deep thought processes. Trudi and Duke looked at him quizzically.

"Unless what sir?" asked Duke. Richens turned towards his Sergeant.

"Has anyone played the recording of Casey speaking on the radio phone-in show to Cellestra Moon yet?" Duke shook his head.

"Not had time yet sir."

"Well get that damn woman over here pronto," demanded Richens as he picked up a marker pen and walked swiftly towards the incident board.

"If I'm not mistaken Duchess, that stuck-up junkie bint Rosie Carmichael just assumed the caller's name was Casey; when really it could have just been his initials, KC," said Richens as he excitedly underlined Kyle Cedel's name on the right hand side of the board; emboldening the letters K and C with a flourish of his pen to illustrate his theory.

"They just can't help themselves," muttered Richens.

"Who?" asked Duke and Jones simultaneously.

"These tarts that anonymously go on the internet," replied Richens.

"There's always something about these nutter keyboard warriors that won't allow them to let go of who they really are; it's as if deep down they're leaving us a trail of cryptic clues and want to get caught." Duke and Jones looked back quizzically.

"They're subconsciously testing us Duchess. Whether they know it or not, they usually leave some clue or other that connects them with the crime. They just can't help themselves." Richens picked up his newspaper that was still folded open at the crossword page.

"Ah, I see sir, a tenuous link so they can some how claim the crime to be theirs and claim their fifteen minutes of fame?" offered Duke helpfully.

"You mean our man Kyle Cedel subconsciously wanted to be associated with the Cellestragate incident, so he used his initials as his name when he spoke to Rosie Carmichael."

"Precisely," replied Richens.

"But why implicate yourself?" asked Trudi, slightly perplexed by the speed at which thoughts ran through the Inspector's mind. Richens turned around and stared at the confused expression on Trudi's face.

"They enjoy the infamy I suppose. Maybe they expect one day they'll be caught and this is their way to claim the credit and wallow in the notoriety of the crime; to say they left intelligent clues all along but the plod were too thick or too slow to spot them? Maybe they're just so fixated on themselves that they need their crime to have some sort of link with their own identity? When you've been on the force as long as me you'll realise the criminal mind is a law unto itself Jones. I don't know why the bloody nutters do it; all I do know is they just can't help themselves."

#

Timeline: Wednesday evening

Lynden Brace had carefully invited the most susceptible of willing participants to attend what he jovially referred to as an 'experiment in mind control.' He had posted an online invitation to his most loyal followers asking them to volunteer to take part in his new TV series that had the working title of 'Fool the Nation.' All of his social media accounts had been inundated with hundreds of enthusiastic fans eager to join their idol on this latest voyage of discovery. Lynden had assessed each applicant thoroughly and now his short-list of fifty malleable volunteers sat before him in the TV studio; in a state of deep hypnosis. They each believed they were simply watching a practice run of the Shimmer Stakes lottery show; a dry-run to test out the new studio setting. They were all blissfully unaware of their role in the deception, as the lights dimmed, the music dropped to a low hum, and four members of a newly launched boy band pulled a big green lever to release the lottery draw balls.

Cellestra had a live feed to the studio where the show was being recorded. Her head ached as she silently watched the flickering monitor screen in her dressing room. The pounding in her temples was relentless, and now her face twitched nervously as the lottery draw machine spat out its life-changing sequence of numbers.

As the last of the six balls landed softly in its cradle, Cellestra drew a large deep breath before taking a slug of cherry brandy to wash down a couple of Paracetamol tablets. She now had the all important six numbers that would save her career, and her daughter. Hurriedly she picked up the pay-as-you-go mobile phone the kidnapper had given to her and entered the six numbers into a text message.

"There you go you fucker," she laughed nervously.

"Think you can get one over Cellestra Moon do you? You spineless bastard," she slurred as she watched the colour of the speech bubble on the phone change to a 'message sent' status.

Cellestra poured out another celebratory measure of cherry brandy into the large balloon glass perched on the dressing table, before slumping back onto one of the cream leather sofas with a deep sigh of relief. Another hurdle in her long career overcome she thought to herself, as a wry self-satisfied smile began to grow across her cherry stained lips. Cellestra's self-indulgent moment was rudely interrupted by a soft knock on her dressing room door.

"Who is it?" asked Cellestra, straightening up from the sofa and pulling her purple and gold shawl around her shoulders.

"It's Lynden Brace. Can I come in?"

"Just a moment," chirped Cellestra as she glanced in the dressing table mirror to check her appearance. Quickly she ran a brush through her short ash blond hair and sprayed a fine mist of perfume over her ample cleavage, before opening the door to greet the man who had just helped to save her reputation and perhaps her daughter's life.

Lynden entered Cellestra's dressing room. He swiftly pulled a pale pink silk handkerchief from his top pocket; quickly covering his nose to avoid the overpowering stench of cherry brandy and strong perfume that clung to the air. Cellestra was oblivious to his subtle action and promptly enveloped him in the sweaty grip of her wobbly arms.

"Lynden" she breathed, pulling him close into her bosom.

"How can I ever thank you enough?"

84

"Well Cellestra . . . I can call you Cellestra can't I?" enquired Lynden coyly. Cellestra nodded and smiled back at him.

"We're not entirely out of the woods yet you know," he continued as he diplomatically peeled away from Cellestra's grasp and sat on the sofa that was furthest away from her. Cellestra looked at him quizzically, as she topped up her brandy balloon and gestured towards the other unused glass to offer Lynden a drink. Lynden smiled and gently shook his head to decline.

"Well, first of all we need to make sure that Saturday night goes smoothly," he continued.

"It's going to be a risky business and the studio bosses have had to grease a few palms to keep the production team on-side, but I think we've got all bases covered."

"What do you mean?" asked Cellestra, the cherry brandy and Paracetamol cocktail now beginning to dull her senses slightly.

Lynden explained how on the following weekend the TV channel was going to deliberately allow its coverage of a live sporting event to over-run. Consequentially the lottery draw show would air fifty minutes later than normally scheduled. This would give the TV company bosses an excuse to send home the audience who had pre-booked tickets for the hour-long live broadcast. The razzmatazz of the usual show wouldn't go ahead. It would be cut short to ten minutes and they would not need so many people in the audience to witness the draw.

The independent moderators, who would oversee the proceedings and manually record the official winning numbers, were also being worked on by the mentalist. Lynden had successfully infiltrated their place of work and, posing as a mental health therapist, he claimed to have created a short series of hypnotherapy sessions which had been designed to relieve stress in the workplace. Lynden convinced his willing guinea pigs to take advantage of the free treatments and, during hypnosis, they had become two more unwitting accomplices to the deception.

On the Saturday evening the adjudicators and Lynden's carefully selected small audience would be led onto a closed

85

set. The celebrity boy band were to be brought back in to make the draw. At the same time the edited pre-recorded ball sequence from earlier in the week would be broadcast as if it were live. On leaving the studio the moderators' records would be switched for the numbers from Wednesday evening's practice run. If either of the officials actually noticed at a later date that the numbers had been changed then they would put this down to their own memory failings. Lynden's careful mind manipulation techniques would ensure his willing volunteers in the audience had been suitably confused by a series of different numbers that were drawn during the mind control event. The winning lottery numbers drawn live on the Saturday evening would be a blur to them. The celebrity pop stars would have been suitably plied with just enough booze and weed to dull their memories. To them it would be just another publicity button push or lever pull, with no more importance than the opening of a new supermarket. To the outside world it would appear as if it was an ordinary lottery draw and nothing was amiss.

"Don't forget," said Lynden as he reached for the door handle to open Cellestra's dressing room door.

"It's really important that you remember to send David out to buy a lottery ticket with those winning numbers on tomorrow, so you'll have the ransom money to pay for Millie's release."

Chapter 8

Timeline: Thursday morning

The next day Cellestra sat nervously fidgeting and fiddling with the braiding on the edge of her gold and purple cashmere shawl as she waited in DI Richens' office. Her feet tapped on the painted concrete floor as she stared around aimlessly at the soulless room and tried to take her mind off her cherry brandy hang over. Duke's wilting spider plant still hung limply across the top of the gunmetal grey filing cabinet in the opposite corner of the room; it probably hadn't been watered for weeks. This only served to remind Cellestra of how thirsty she was feeling and now, in this God forsaken early hour of the morning, her pounding headache had returned.

DS Duke entered the room carrying two cups of spring water that were precariously balanced on top of a stack of manila folders. Cellestra reached up to relieve Duke of the two cool plastic cups and placed them on the desk. He nodded his thanks and placed the folders next to the parched spider plant on top of the cabinet before dragging a chair over to sit opposite Cellestra.

"Thank you for coming in to the station so early Ms Moon," said Duke. Cellestra gulped down one of the cups of water to quench her thirst.

"I have something I need you to listen to." DS Duke flicked a switch on a CD player on his desk and immediately the recording of a radio phone-in show began to play Kyle Cedel's voice.

"I believe she hears voices from the other side alright; the other side of the auditorium."

Cellestra recognised the voice immediately as the kidnapper with the chilling lisping whisper on the phone. She felt her body freeze, as if a shock of electricity had stung straight through her. She felt her stomach churn and her joints fizz as a layer of sweat enveloped the whole of her body. She tried to rise up off her seat but her legs began to wobble uneasily beneath her. Unable to gain her balance, Cellestra slapped back down onto the hard plastic chair.

"That's him," she croaked, reaching out for the other plastic cup of water. Duke passed it to her and she immediately gulped down the cooling liquid before crunching the cup onto the metal desk. Cellestra wiped the back of her wrist across her top lip to soak up the sweat and moustache of water that had splashed up from the cup, before turning to Duke and shouting:

"You've got him. That's the bastard who is trying to ruin my life."

#

Timeline: Saturday afternoon

Millie was exhausted from the effort of trying to locate the shiny piece of metal on the factory floor. She was sure she had seen it glinting in the shaft of sunlight from the roof, but she hadn't eaten for days and she was now beginning to wonder if it had been in her imagination. The occasional visits from her captors to bring her protein shakes had been rather spasmodic. She had lost all track of time and her muscles were growing weaker. She began to shiver as she slumped back against the cold factory wall again. Her relaxed buttocks slapped hard onto the factory floor as mercifully the twine around her neck slackened. Startled by the sudden noise, a sparrow took flight from its perch on the mezzanine balcony above her and flapped out through the hole in the roof to freedom.

'Right you shiny little bastard. Let's give it one more try,' thought a determined Millie. Her heels grappled around in the oily dust, feeling for the small piece of metal that she hoped lay somewhere on the floor nearby. Suddenly she could feel something sharp scratch the edge of her right foot. She shuffled around, frantically scraping her bound ankles over the grimy surface. Then, in the dirty black carpet of factory dust, she could feel the cold sharp point of a six-inch nail pressing into the side of her foot.

'Oh my God, I've found it,' she screamed to herself, as she gently wedged the nail between her heels.

'Don't panic, don't panic. Take it easy.' She wanted to drag it towards her waiting outstretched fingers, but her legs were still bound straight together with the wooden splint. She knew the only way she would be able to move the nail was if she could break the pole and bend her knees again. Reluctantly she let the nail drop back onto the floor. Gradually she rolled over onto her right thigh and slowly yet purposefully began to flex her knees, swinging her tethered legs to-and-fro. Again and again she tried, twisting, flexing and rolling; until she heard a very small cracking sound. The wooden pole had begun to weaken. Relentlessly she carried on, flexing and twisting, rolling around on the dirt encrusted concrete floor. Suddenly she felt the wood split. With one final swift jerk of her knees she pulled her feet up towards her buttocks, forcing the wooden pole to splinter at the centre. At last she could bend her legs.

Exhausted Millie lay back against the slimy cold wall again, trying to catch her breath through the gagging rag that was still taped inside her mouth. But she couldn't stop now, she'd come this far; she had to locate the nail again before the kidnappers came back. She shuffled back down into the black sooty dust and began scraping her feet over the concrete floor. Suddenly she felt the familiar cold sharp stab of the nail pressing into the heel of her right foot. Slowly she positioned her feet astride the nail and wedged it between her heels, before pulling it towards her. Carefully she turned around to bring her tethered hands closer to the nail. Gingerly she stretched out her fingers and scratched through the dust to pick up the precious piece of metal. Millie allowed herself a small sigh of relief as she jostled the nail in the palm of her hand before carefully positioning it between the thumb and forefinger of her right hand.

Excitedly she started to blindly jab and prod the nail into the thick tape that bound her wrists together. Beginning with a small hole at one end, she started to perforate the tape; methodically working her way through the black sticky wadding. Occasionally stopping to test for signs of weakness in the bindings, Millie continued to work with the nail. She carried on for what seemed like endless hours, prodding, tugging and

89

twisting until eventually, just as dusk fell through the skylight, she felt a sudden tear and the welcome feeling of release. Her wrists sprang freely forward in front of her. Immediately she pulled away the tape from her mouth, spitting out the dirty rag that had silenced her terror and let out a gasp of air. Quickly she wrenched the tape from her legs and ankles to remove the splintered wooden pole, then slowly and very carefully she prised open the knot in the twine around her neck to slip the noose over her head. The final release from her bondage was now complete. Millie stood up from the floor. She was free.

#

Timeline: Saturday early evening

Kyle Cedel relaxed on the single bed in the modest sanctuary of his scruffy rented bed-sit. The previous tenant had been evicted just the day before, so Kyle had spent most of the day clearing a mountain of detritus left by the former occupier. He had changed the bedding, washed down the surfaces, vacuumed the floor and hung his favourite fantasy film poster on the wall to hide a piece of missing plaster. Dozens of empty beer cans, take-away cartons and porn magazines left by the last tenant had all been neatly stacked into colour coded refuse sacks ready for recycling the next day. However, despite all of this industrious housework, a cloying odour of nicotine and damp dog clung to the heavily stained carpet. But Kyle didn't mind. A thin watery smile appeared across his pasty face as he began to set up his TV in time for that evening's lottery draw.

#

As a cool early evening breeze stirred through the hole in the factory roof, an exhausted Millie felt a chill crawl over her flesh. Hugging herself closely, she gazed into the darkness that enveloped the deserted building, before slowly feeling her way to the corner of the unit. In the semi-darkness, she carefully climbed a wrought iron spiral staircase that led up to the floor above. The cold edges of the metal grilles bit sharply into her bare feet making Millie wince with pain as she continued to shuffle along the gridding.

The mezzanine balcony stretched around each wall of the factory, like a minstrel's gallery, and it had indeed once served as a source of entertainment for the lads on the factory floor. In years gone by, many a blue collar had looked up from his assembly line to gaze in awe through the grid at the delights hidden beneath a personal assistant's Lycra micro skirt. The secretaries were oblivious to this embarrassing fact until someone let it slip to one poor girl that they preferred the black panties she had worn yesterday instead of the pink ones she was wearing today.

Eventually Millie reached an office at the end of the metal gridded walkway. She softly pushed open the cracked glazed door and peered inside. Her eyes had become accustomed to the darkness but it was still difficult to see clearly. She made her way inside the room and stumbled into a large wooden desk, catching her right thigh on the sharp corner of the furniture. Millie let out a small cry and placed a hand on the desktop to steady herself. She smiled inwardly as she discovered a small box of matches beneath her outstretched fingers. Immediately she opened the carton and lit one of the matches to illuminate the small office space.

Rubber bands and pencils spilled out of an over-turned desk tidy. A collection of yellow stained newspapers were scattered over the floor where a dismissed employee, in defiance of his unwelcome redundancy, had urinated as a parting gift to the management. A stale odour clung to the walls and the dank air seemed still and ageless; as if she had wandered into a time capsule. Millie didn't notice the match was about to burn into her fingertips until it was too late. She winced with the shock of the hot pain but immediately she lit another. Suddenly a wave of relief washed over her, as her dry lips cracked open into a still beautiful smile; because there, in the half-light of the small office, she had found what she had been looking for. Hanging limply on a single metal hook that had been screwed lazily into the plaster wall, were a forgotten pair of dusty dark blue overalls and a discarded baseball cap.

91

Millie quickly slipped into the clothes and scrunched her matted hair up into the hat. Next she unrolled the wads of thick tape that were still around her wrists and one of her legs, carefully flattening them and dividing them into two equal halves. Then she began to criss-cross the duct tape around each foot, to make a crude pair of slippers.

"There!" she said triumphantly, as in the half-light of the moon, they looked just like flat plimsolls. Maybe now she could slip outside, largely unnoticed in a crowd of twilight shift workers. After all she didn't know who or where her kidnappers were; Millie could trust no one. She would only feel safe once she was back in the sanctuary of her parents' protection.

#

Timeline: Saturday late evening

Kyle Cedel stared blankly at his TV screen in total disbelief. His anger raged through his whole gingery body, like the glowing magma from a volcanic eruption.

"What the fuck is this bollocks?" His usual softly spoken voice rose to a pitched scream as he punched a key on his mobile phone to dial a stored number.

The late night newscaster had just introduced an exclusive report that they had proof Cellestra Moon had successfully predicted that night's winning lottery numbers. They were interviewing a young girl called Avani Kapoor. She worked on the till at her father's grocery shop. The pretty raven-haired shop assistant remembered selling Cellestra Moon a lottery ticket a couple of days before.

"I thought well, if those numbers are good enough for Cellestra Moon, then they're good enough for me," giggled Avani nervously.

"So I bought a ticket with the same numbers on," she continued. The young shop girl smiled sweetly into the camera and firmly gripped her jackpot winning lottery ticket.

After leaving the police station Cellestra's head had been in a tailspin from hearing the kidnapper's voice on Duke's CD player. Her headache had got much worse. She had called into a

92

mini-mart shop on her way back to the studio to buy a box of pain killers. Once at the counter she had half remembered what Lynden had said about not forgetting to buy a lottery ticket, so she had added that to her basket of items at the checkout. Avani told the pack of reporters that Cellestra had also bought a prawn mayo sandwich, some bars of chocolate, a couple of bottles of Cherry Brandy, a newspaper and a couple of boxes of Paracetamol tablets.

The TV news reporter's closing piece to camera said there had been four jackpot winners that evening; the girl from the newsagent's shop in Hanford and three other people whose identities were as yet unknown. But Avani Kapoor was adamant that one of the unknown winners would be Cellestra Moon.

Kyle Cedel waited for the phone to auto-dial. After a few rings Cellestra Moon croakily answered the call.

The unwelcome sharp trill of Cellestra's personal mobile phone had roused the Psychic from her drunken stupor. The stress of the past week had taken its toll and she had sought to find relief inside yet another bottle of booze. David has decided to leave his drunken wreck of a wife to sleep it off in her dressing room while he anxiously waited for the next contact from the kidnappers in the sanctuary of his own office.

"You know who I am," Kyle Cedel's unrushed tone returned, as a wry smile came to the lips of the softly spoken man.

"Listen to me carefully Carol Frogson," spat Kyle. Cellestra froze with panic as she suddenly realised the kidnapper wasn't calling her on the usual pay-as-you-go mobile phone; he had her private number.

"Both you and I know your lucky lottery prediction isn't due to any psychic ability, you fat-arsed hag" he continued, his lisping speech impediment becoming more pronounced with each shot of anger running through his words.

"You weren't supposed to use this exercise as a PR stunt you fucking retard. It was meant to teach you a lesson." Although menacing, Kyle's sinister voice was calm and even as he put great effort into controlling his temper. Cellestra remained speechless.

"If you ever want to see your spoilt brat of a daughter alive again, then you're going to have to confess right now, live on the TV news you stinking bitch. You've got one hour to go on and tell everyone I am right and you've just fucking scammed the whole country you fat fucking waste of air. One hour or your kid dies."

Click, the line went dead.

#

"So, you know we got that positive ID on the voice sir and Cellestra Moon confirmed that Rosie Carmichael's Casey, AKA Kyle Cedel, is the same voice as the kidnapper's . . ." DS Duke was summarising the facts and hurriedly bringing his boss up to date with the latest developments in the case.

". . . well, for the past two days uniform have been watching the home address that Trudi came up with for Cedel. It's a run down B&B but he's a no show." Richens remained silently deep in thought. In the experienced police officer's mind something didn't quite add up.

The kidnapper was using pay-as-you-go phones which made tracing them an extremely difficult task. The police could only triangulate a signal from the phones when they were switched on, and the kidnapper had been careful to ensure he always switched off his phone immediately after using it. If Kyle Cedel didn't return to his registered home address, then it was going to be a very tiresome and drawn-out process to find him. That aside, Richens just could not shake the uneasy feeling he had about the woman with red hair who had handed the package to Cellestra Moon at the meet and greet. Where had she gone? People couldn't just disappear into thin air. Despite days of scrutinising all of the CCTV recordings, the mysterious red haired woman could not be traced anywhere on any of the other recordings taken before or after the hand-over of the package. She was seen leaving the merchandising stand and heading towards a service corridor. The only other people seen in the corridor on the next consecutive camera were crew members and celebrities.

DI Richens needed to clear his head. He pulled open the top drawer of his desk to retrieve his copy of the Times newspaper that had been folded down to expose his half completed crossword. Duke watched in annoyance as his boss appeared to be reacting quite nonchalantly to the day's developments. Richens ran a closed hand over his stubbly chin, a watery smile began to grow beneath his thin pointed nose, as he looked across at Duke.

"You know what Duchess," said Richens.

"I think I'm just about to crack this puzzle. I can feel it in my bones." Just then Richens' attention was drawn to the muted TV screen on the far wall of the CID office.

"What the fuck is that all about?" he asked indignantly. Duke spun around in his office chair to watch the rolling news, quickly grabbing the remote control to turn up the sound on the distant TV. The news station was running the same ticker-tape report it had been running throughout the evening that Cellestra Moon had successfully predicted that night's winning lottery numbers. Avani Kapoor was standing outside her father's grocery shop, smiling at the cameras with her winning ticket firmly gripped in her hand

"What the hell is that Moon woman playing at?" growled Richens.

"Is that thick northern bint really that stupid? Publicity like this will spook the kidnapper and blow the whole case wide open." Duke watched his boss return to his desk. Richens was shaking his head in disbelief at the Psychic's thoughtless action.

95

Chapter 9

Timeline: Saturday late night

Millie knew that her captors could return at any time and she needed to find a way out of the abandoned factory unit. The only door to the outside world she had seen was the heavy metal one that had been bolted and locked from the outside by the two men when they left. 'There must be another exit somewhere,' she thought. Millie walked out of the office and gingerly made her way back across the mezzanine balcony and down the spiral staircase. She winced at sharp pains in her feet as the crude duct tape slippers afforded little protection from the biting metal grille. Quickly she crossed the floor of the factory towards a wooden door in an unexplored corner of the unit. Millie lit another match. She could make out the picture on the door looked like a simple line drawing of a man. She pushed the door open and peered inside the room. A heavy stench of sewage and stagnant water crawled into her nostrils. Millie had found the gents' toilets. She took a step back out into the factory to take a breath of air and suddenly had the uneasy feeling that she was not alone.

#

Cellestra Moon emerged through the stage door. Gone were the cheers and squeals of joy from her usual adoring public; gone was the carefully choreographed session of chatting with her excited fans. Instead, Cellestra had left the hazy sanctuary of her dressing room stupor to be greeted by an almost hostile wall of flashing lights, jabbing cameras and poking microphones. She wouldn't remember who asked the first fateful question as, just like her fans, all reporters looked pretty much the same to Cellestra. But one small, anonymous voice was about to completely change the life of Cellestra Moon forever.

"Ms Moon. What do you say to the person who claims he has evidence that you and the TV production company staged the whole of tonight's Shimmer Stakes lottery draw, you didn't predict the numbers and you are indeed a fake?"

"Did you buy a ticket?"

"What are you going to do with the money?" The questions just kept firing.

Cellestra took in a deep breath and held onto the stage door hand rail to steady herself at the top of the concrete steps. Smiling weakly she gazed out at the assembled gaggle of reporters; her midnight inquisition. It was as if every small twitch on her face set off a domino of flashing cameras.

"It wasn't me," she whispered, shielding her eyes from the hot glare of the blazing lights. A collective gasp came from the group as more cameras clicked.

"What wasn't you?" enquired an authoritative sounding voice from the front.

"Is it true? Did you predict the lottery numbers or not?" came the defining question.

"I suppose in a way" slurred a confused Cellestra. A large tear began to roll down her hot flushed face. The reporters continued to fire more questions at the bewildered woman, as she desperately tried to hold off the inevitable moment when she would have to admit to the world that she was a fake.

"It wasn't what I wanted" she slurred, drunkenly waving her wobbly bingo-winged arms at the crowd.

"It was all a lie." Cellestra buried her face in her hands as the bank of paparazzi cameras systematically flashed back at her.

"They made me go along with it, but it was all a lie; a show," she slurred, wiping her fingers down her puffy cheeks. The gathered mob was momentarily silenced by the unexpectedly frank response; all of them secretly hoping their patience would be rewarded by more revelations from the drunken woman. Knowing that she now had the reporters' full attention, Cellestra lifted up her head, sniffed defiantly and purposefully wiped away the tears beneath her eyes, before looking squarely into lens of the nearest TV camera.

"Are you happy now? Are you fucking happy now?" ranted Cellestra, launching into a cherry brandy fuelled tirade.

"I'm nothing but a bloody fra . . ." Suddenly she felt a pair of strong hands grab her shoulders, pulling her back inside the building, cutting her off in mid sentence. The stage door firmly slammed shut behind her.

"What the bloody hell are you doing?" barked Lynden Brace as he looked down at the broken, brandy-soaked woman that stood in front of him. They could both hear the shouting reporters outside still scratching and whining like a pack of wolves at the door, trying to get in to extract every last drop of blood from their prey. Cellestra gazed up at him as he pulled a pale pink silk handkerchief from his waistcoat pocket and began to use it to wipe tears away from her red sore eyes.

"I'm sorry," she blubbed. Lynden remained silent, carefully dabbing away her salty tears.

"After all your hard work," she cried, pulling herself into his chest. He saw her eyes begin to well up with more tears; a whole tsunami of sorrow that seemed to dampen the very fire in her soul.

"It's all true, I am a fraud. I am not psychic. I'm a fake, a big fat fake. I always have been," she sobbed. Lynden gave her an awkward hug as he gently patted the back of her head.

"I know," he said blankly.

"Everyone knows really," he whispered gently. Cellestra started to sniff back tears.

"But what's happened Cellestra? What are the press hounding you for? Today of all days?" quizzed Lynden.

Cellestra stared back up into his beady hawk-like eyes that were firmly locked onto her face. She knew she had nowhere to hide. It was only a matter of time before the mentalist discovered her stupid, selfish hung over mistake. Cellestra began to cry uncontrollably as she blubbed out the words that Lynden simply hadn't expected to hear.

"The kidnapper called me and said he saw on the news that I bought a winning lottery ticket," she sniffled.

"And now he's angry with me because it makes me look like a real genuine Psychic. So he's told the newspapers about it."

Cellestra dropped to her knees and began to frantically pound her fists on the corridor wall.

"Oh God, oh God, it's all over for me isn't it? My life is over. Everything I've worked for is gone." She sobbed.

"And now he's going to kill her isn't he? He's going to kill my baby girl."

The fact that Cellestra's outburst had been primarily focussed on her own downfall rather than the fate of her daughter went momentarily unnoticed by Lynden, as he felt a sudden flash of panic wash over his whole body. A stab of fear and anger wove simultaneously through his chest. 'What the fuck had this stupid fat delusional cow gone and done now?' he thought. She only had one simple job to do, just text the winning lottery numbers to the kidnapper ahead of the draw. It was David who should go out and anonymously buy a winning ticket. But instead of following Lynden's perfect plan, Cellulite Moo had gone totally off-piste and blown the whole well orchestrated plot out of the water. 'Why the hell had she bought the sodding ticket herself? Why hadn't she stuck to the plan? How was the showman ever going to pull back from this?'

Lynden frantically ran his hands through his shiny purple-black hair as if trying to pluck an idea from his brain. He looked down at Cellestra who had slumped down onto the concrete floor crying; the pack of hungry wolves still scratching at the door behind her. He took in a deep purposeful breath to regain his composure and ran the fingertips of his right hand through the hairs of his smartly clipped goatee beard. A thousand thoughts whirred through his mind as he bent down to help Cellestra to her feet.

"Come on you," he said calmly with a feigned reassuring smile.

"Let's get you back to your dressing room."

Lynden helped Cellestra as she shuffled through the short maze of concrete corridors. As they arrived at the door to the star's dressing room Cellestra seemed to be falling into drunken unconsciousness. Lynden had almost carried her all the way from the stage door. Her heavy bulk had taken its toll on the slightly built man. When they arrived at Cellestra's door Lynden was panting with exhaustion. Carefully he propped her up against the door frame and slowly turned the handle. Almost immediately Cellestra slumped to the side and fell through the open doorway, landing with a heavy thump on the cream rug. Cellestra groaned as the jolt seemed to momentarily bring her out of her stupor.

Lynden could see the utter hopelessness on Cellestra's face as, like an upturned giant sea turtle, it appeared impossible for her to get herself up off the floor. He offered her his hand and helped to lever her bulky body up onto one of the sofas.

"Thanks Lyn," slurred Cellestra, holding the side of her temple. Lynden ignored the irritation he felt by the unnecessary shortening of his name.

"Do you need a tablet or something for that headache?" he asked. She nodded and pointed to a small assortment of pills on the dressing table. Lynden picked up a bottle of Paracetamol tablets and unscrewed the child-proof lid before placing it in Cellestra's eager hand.

"Try to get some sleep Cellestra," he said as he stood up and left the room, quietly closing the door behind him.

"Don't you worry, Mummy will make it all better for you; you just wait and see," babbled Cellestra as she unscrewed the cap on a new bottle of Cherry Brandy.

#

Timeline: Sunday morning 1.00am

Millie closed her eyes and shivered as she summoned the courage to go back into the toilet block. She had no choice as it was the only area of the dank soulless factory that she hadn't fully explored. She still needed to find a way out; a door, a window, anything that would enable her to break free. This was her last hope. As she lit another match she could make out the glinting pairs of beady eyes watching her every move from the other end of a row of broken urinals. This was where the colony of rats had entered the building from the sewers. She was aware that this was the rodent army's territory and she would need to tread carefully to avoid any confrontation.

'Pull yourself together girl,' thought Millie. She slowly picked her way through the moving wave of brown and black fur that chattered and squeaked at her feet. Eventually she arrived at an old stainless steel sink unit at the end of the room; above it was a small metal framed window. The glass was frosted to obscure the view from the outside world and it was closed shut with a rusty catch and handle. Millie prayed it would open as she was sure this would be her only chance of escape. She took in a deep breath, the foul stench from the sewers clung inside her nose and throat. The choking girl climbed on top of the sink and desperately pulled at the latch but the window frame had been painted shut. The colony of rats tauntingly squealed and jostled around the base of the sink; as if entertained by her valiant attempt.

"Come on you bastard," shouted an exhausted Millie as she continued to push around the window frame.

"Just give me a fucking break."

After a few moments she felt the catch release and the ripping sound of dried-on paint giving way, as the top pane suddenly flung ajar. A welcome breeze of fresh air flowed in through the opening. With no time to think Millie squeezed through the narrow open window and slid down the outside wall to freedom. She had escaped.

Millie turned up the collar on her workman's overalls and pulled the baseball cap down securely. She put her hands in the deep side pockets of the boiler suit and a broad smile enveloped her face as she discovered a handful of discarded change inside.

#

Timeline: Sunday morning 2:45am

David Moon had waited nervously by his mobile phone for hours, he now felt as if the small silver handset was permanently attached to his body. The other pay-as-you-go handset from the kidnappers sat tauntingly silent on his desk. Occasionally he would pick up both phones and check the displays just to make sure he hadn't gone temporarily deaf and missed a call. In other moments of paranoia he would call the mobiles from his landline, just to check the lines were still connected. His wife had taken to drowning her depression in a bottle of Cherry Brandy each night and had become totally incapable of rational thought at any hour of the day. David had decided if the kidnapper was going to call with instructions then he would be the more rational parent to deal with the arrangements. Also, if Millie ever managed to escape from her captors, he would never forgive himself if she tried to call and couldn't get any sense out of her drunken mother. Millie was a sensible girl; and she knew her father would always cope better in a crisis; that is why he had always ensured she knew his mobile number off by heart. He kept both handsets firmly in sight.

It was nearly three o'clock in the morning. David walked over to the small kitchenette at the end of his office to prepare a fresh cafetiere of coffee. Sleep was a luxury he would not voluntarily consider. 'What would happen if Millie called and I missed her 'cos I was in the land of nod' he'd thought, and consequently he had resigned himself to taking only the briefest of cat naps in his office chair. Surprised at the late hour, he yawned loudly with a forceful stretch of one arm as he poured boiling water over some freshly ground coffee beans.

"It's been a long night," said Lynden Brace standing in the doorway. David spun around.

"Oh hi Lynden, yes, you can say that again. Crikey you're here late aren't you?" David gestured towards the cafetiere to offer Lynden a drink.

"Yes, it's been a long night. I couldn't just go home and sleep after what we managed to pull off this evening, so I thought I'd be better off hanging around here for a while," said Lynden, warmly accepting the offer of a freshly brewed coffee.

"I must admit though, I'd have thought you'd have been outside when Cellestra made her unexpected appearance to the press,"

"What appearance?" asked David.

"Cellestra was pissed again when I left her earlier. She looked like she was about to pick another drunken fight with me and I didn't fancy trying to corral her into the car to get her home, so I left her in the dressing room to sleep it off and came back to my office just after the lottery show went out," added David dozily.

"I was so knackered mate that I just accidentally dozed off at my desk for a couple of minutes. So what appearance are you talking about?" David yawned. Lynden stared at him silently and then lowered his gaze to the floor.

"What announcement Lynden? What has Cellestra done?" asked David, now fully awake.

Lynden opened his mouth to speak but suddenly the awkward silence was broken by the sharp trill of a telephone perched on the work surface next to the coffee machine. An unrecognised 0800 number flashed in the caller display on David's mobile. He immediately picked up the call.

"Hullo? David Moon here."

"Hello, this is the Reverse Line Operator," announced a highly efficient sounding female voice.

"Will you accept a reverse charge call from a Miss Millie Moon?" David's heart felt frozen with panic and relief as the next voice he heard at the end of the line was Millie's.

"Daddy? Is that you Daddy?"

David felt as if his heart would burst on hearing the beautiful sound of that sweet voice. Lynden saw a huge smile envelope David's face.

"Yes Millie, it's me. Where are you darling?" Lynden looked quizzically at David, wondering if what he was imagining was really true. Had Millie managed to escape her kidnapper? Had she been set free? More importantly to Lynden how would this affect his future? The self-assured showman suddenly felt a slight wave of panic crawl through his body.

David started to scribble down what Millie had told him. She was in an old call box on an industrial estate. She could see a faded painted wooden sign at the entrance to the estate that gave a small clue as to her whereabouts. Lynden looked on from the other side of the desk and saw the words 'Blackwater Lane' scrawled across the notepaper in David's tight grasp.

"Just stay there and don't move darling. I'm coming for you straight away." David ended the call and slid his phone into his jacket pocket.

"She's free," he shouted excitedly as he punched a celebratory fist into the air.

"Millie's free," his voice pitching higher and higher.

"I've got to tell Ce," he added.

"No, there's no time for that," cried Lynden.

"Just go and get Millie now!"

"Cellestra's totally out of it at the moment, you'd just be wasting precious time trying to rouse her," he floundered, trying to find the right words to express the urgency of the situation to David.

"You go and get your little girl back. You call the police on the way and I'll tell Cellestra what's happened; you just go and get Millie." Lynden gave him a reassuringly hearty man hug, as David placed the piece of paper in his pocket, grabbed his car keys and raced for the door.

Lynden Brace had never panicked in his life before. Panic was indeed an alien concept to the mentalist. Everything in his neat orderly world was calculated and measured to the very last degree. He enjoyed being the self-proclaimed master of his own destiny. He relished the thought of always being in control of every possible outcome of any possible scenario that his life may encounter. Before making any decision, his mind would automatically assess how he would deal with any repercussions that may occur. This trait was a symptom of his ever-growing obsessive compulsive disorder, a dysfunctional family trait that had always affected his life greatly.

Even the simplest of choices in his orderly life had to be thoroughly calculated and risk assessed. When choosing what to eat at dinner with friends, Lynden would constantly weight up what difference it would make if he had the garlic mushrooms or the Italian tomato soup starter. Would he later have the chance of a romantic kiss that would be scuppered by spicy breath? Or if he had the soup, how likely was it that some would spill down his tie? Would a tomato stained tie put off a prospective romantic conquest more than the stench of garlic? Assessing such scenarios in such great painful detail often led to Lynden opting for the safer more predictable choices in his personal life, such as a plain green salad.

Lynden Brace ran as fast as his shiny pointed-toe leather boots would allow. The showman's winkle picker footwear bit hard into his feet as he raced through the maze of concrete corridors. His usual controlled demeanour gone; his calm and collected appearance now totally dishevelled as he galloped back towards Cellestra Moon's dressing room. He was unable to believe the incredible news that he was about to break to the Medium. Her daughter was alive and free.

The idea that Millie would escape her captor was not a scenario that Lynden had anticipated in his plan to 'Fool the Nation.' He absolutely believed that after the ransom money had been paid he would see front page headlines across the national press reporting that Millie's body had been discovered somewhere. After all, kidnappers were not the most honourable of people and not many of them stuck to their side of the bargain once they had received their spoils of war. Of course he could not openly suggest this to Cellestra and David as a possible outcome. Instead he had chosen to give them the false hope that 'of course their daughter would be safely returned to them after the money was handed over.' Millie had escaped her captor; she would soon be enveloped in the warm safety of her step-father's arms. This unexpected turn of events had sent an unfamiliar wave of panic shooting through Lynden's body, causing him to feel slightly nauseous.

His shiny leather soles skidded to an abrupt halt, as he burst open Cellestra's dressing room door. He stood there panting and wheezing in the doorway, trying to regain his usual self-assured composure. Lynden could see Cellestra's heavy set frame slumped awkwardly across one of the cream leather sofas. One of her diamante slippers had been clumsily kicked off and now lay next to one of her pudgy white feet. Her purple and gold shawl lay strewn across the back of the sofa and he could see a large brandy glass had fallen from her drunken grasp. It now lay on the floor on its side. A small puddle of cherry brandy had collected in the bottom of the balloon and it had begun to dribble out onto the cream rug.

Lynden shook his head in quiet disgust at Cellestra's bulk. She was wearing a pair of grey track-suit bottoms that only just managed to stretch over her doughy thighs. Her crumpled T-shirt had risen up to expose the mountainous fleshy blubber of her dimpled stomach. He could just make out the sweaty stained band of her flesh coloured support bra beneath, that now cut into the fold of fat above her belly. Her head tilted forward as her shiny round face was supported by two double chins that now rested awkwardly on her chest. Lynden noticed a long strand of cherry tinted saliva had collected in the folds of skin around her mouth. An empty plastic pill bottle lay discarded on the cushion next to her.

Slowly he walked over to Cellestra's limp body and lifted her left hand. He could not feel a pulse. Swiftly he pulled a small silver mirror from his waistcoat pocket and placed it in front of Cellestra's mouth and nose. He could see no breath on the glass. Quietly, in the sanctuary of Cellestra's dressing room, Lynden pondered when he should dial 999. He knew he had to carefully think how best to handle the unexpected situation. He knew that it would be one life-changing call that would kick-start an unstoppable juggernaut of events; a media circus that would eventually announce to the waiting world that the country's most adored Medium was dead.

#

During his journey to Blackwater Lane, David had tried to phone Cellestra to give her the fantastic news that their daughter was free; but his numerous attempts to call his drunken wife had been diverted to voicemail. He had then dialled 999 and the handler immediately dispatched a fleet of rapid response police cars and an ambulance to meet him at the industrial estate. Lashing rain pounded against David's car windscreen as he slowly drove around the industrial estate searching for Millie. The glass began to fog up again as his wipers vainly beat against the heavy summer downpour. He had been driving around for almost half an hour and the early dawn mist had fallen hypnotically onto his heavy, sore eyelids. The fan vents were turned up to maximum and the torrent of humid air was now beginning to make him feel even more sleepy. Somewhere in the back streets he could hear the distant wail of police sirens.

106

"Where the hell are you?" muttered David, his eyes scanning each and every roller shutter door. He checked the hastily written address he had jotted down when Millie had called, just to confirm in his own mind he was in the right location. The distant sirens were growing closer now and he prayed he hadn't led the whole posse on a wild goose chase.

"Come on baby, where are you?" David's car crawled down another alleyway, passing more rows of anonymous looking starter units. He had no idea that Blackwater Lane was such a hive of industrial activity, or how many people were gainfully employed in these anonymously regimented brick and steel boxes. The stench of engine oil hung heavily in the air as more rain danced on the bonnet of David's car. As he turned the final corner an old public telephone box came into view. Through the misty beams of his car headlights, David could just make out the ragged silhouette of a dark figure dressed in heavy workman's overalls and wearing a baseball cap. The figure crouched and shivered on the floor of the telephone kiosk. Slowly David drew up alongside and wound down the window to get a better view. The unrelenting rain continually spat into the car, instantly soaking David's hair and jacket.

Millie slowly rolled her head to one side and opened her heavy, salty eyes to peer through the grimy bottom pane of the telephone box. It felt to David as if his heart had somersaulted into his mouth as he flung open the car door and ran to gather her into his arms. The search party of blue flashing lights drew closer, their sirens blasting an almost victorious salute.

"Millie," he wept as they rocked to-and-fro in the rainy half-light of the early morning.

"My God I thought we'd lost you."

#

Despite her harrowing ordeal at the hands of her captors, Millie had refused to go to hospital with the paramedics; she was desperate to see her parents and to take comfort in the safe and familiar arms of David Moon. At that moment in time he was her saviour; the only person she believed she could trust. Her physical injuries were superficial compared with the deep

107

psychological damage inflicted by the kidnappers and she needed the warmth of her father's embrace to make her feel safe. As they sat in the back of a police car Millie buried herself in David's fatherly hugs. Millie needed answers to come to terms with why this had happened to her. She knew that her parents were the only people who would be able to help her make sense of it all.

"Where's Mom?" asked Millie, snuggling her tear-stained face into David's chest.

"She's waiting for you my love, don't worry," he replied, embarrassed by the fact that his wife had been too drunk to stay awake long enough to wait for news of her daughter. He only hoped to God that Lynden Brace had been able to rouse Cellestra from her drunken stupor to give her the good news and sober her up in time for a family reunion.

"She'll meet us at the police station later," he added reassuringly.

Millie straightened up and pulled away from him; a small frown grew across her tired face.

"I need to ask you something," she continued, staring directly into her father's eyes.

"What's that darling?" soothed David, as he gently pulled her close again.

"Is Mom a fake?"

Chapter 10

Timeline: Sunday morning 8.30am

DS Duke's migraine was the heavy price he was paying for another stressful case. It didn't seem to make any difference how long he'd worked in CID, he would never allow himself to become anaesthetised to the many gruelling images he saw on a now weekly basis. He would never allow the horrifying reports of kidnappings, rapes, murder and mutilations to become second nature to him. His current migraine was not about to let him forget that Millie Moon could easily become the subject of the next post-mortem report to land on his desk.

Millie's kidnapping had played heavily on his mind all night. Imagining her frightened, innocent pleas for mercy had weaved their way through his consciousness; envisaging her absolute terror at the hands of her captor; images of her terrified face had burst directly into his brain. The photographs of the mutilated lifeless body of the man found in Witches' Wood constantly flickered in his memory. Right now DS Duke was staring down at a sanitised toilet cubicle floor, his head in his hands. After a largely sleepless night Duke had come into work early. His mobile battery was dead so, before going to his office, he decided to take advantage of a small uninterrupted moment alone with his thoughts and slipped into the gents' toilets. The weary sergeant was trying to escape the hustle and bustle of the Police station, the constant trill of an informant's telephone call, the beep of more incoming email and the whirring hum of the office printer. During the past week he had also had to negotiate a constant stream of interviews with self-proclaimed psychics who, despite the media blackout, somehow knew about the kidnapping and had offered their services. Many were convinced that Millie Moon was dead. The pounding thud that continually thumped in his head felt like it was performing a duet with a pulsing steel metal band; a band that continually tightened its unrelenting grip over his temples with every heartbeat.

"Yo Duchess!" interrupted Richens suddenly, as he rattled on the flimsy cubicle door.

"You dropping the kids off at the pool in there or what?" Duke was not in the mood for early morning copper's banter and simply got to his feet, flushed the toilet and opened the door.

"What's the problem?" he asked as he washed his hands.

"Haven't you head the news Duchess?" replied Richens excitedly.

"God man, where have you been?" continued the inspector, without waiting for a reply.

"Millie Moon turned up in the early hours of this morning. She looks like shit but the Doc reckons she's physically okay." A shallow smile washed over Duke's relieved tired face.

"You mean she's alive?" asked Duke.

"Yeah mate, it looks a bit like she's been through the wringer but yeah, she's safe and well in the SAS room," replied Richens.

"Mind you, I reckon there's a whole load more to this than meets the eye though Duchess." Duke looked back quizzically at his babbling boss.

"Well, Daddy dearest has been spilling the Moon's secrets all over the shop. It looks like Cellestra Moon, or should I say Carol Frogson, was being pretty cagey about her dodgy past and there's some nasty stuff about Millie's biological father that we didn't know about before." Duke dried his hands on a paper towel and felt his headache begin to lift with the relief that the girl was safe.

"Are you coming in on this or what?" added Richens with a cheery whistle as he led the way ahead of Duke out of the gents' toilets and back down the corridor.

#

Millie sank back into the soft orange sofa cushions and hugged the Styrofoam coffee cup into her chest, staring down intently at the frothy Cappuccino. The Serious Assault Suite had an atmosphere of anonymous security, yet it seemed to Millie that it only served to create a heightened state of limbo for its clientele. No going forward without first going back. But then no one was going to rush Millie into going back to re-live her terrifying ordeal of the past seven days. That had to be done in her own time, at her own pace, on her own terms.

A uniformed female PC sat next to Millie, giving a well-trained reassuring smile. Her role was as a chaperone for the scared teenager; a supporting hand to hold. Millie warmed to her guardian. There was no pressure, there were no awkward questions, no pushing. Instead the woman patiently sat on the sofa waiting for the young girl to speak.

It was the cold light of morning and Millie knew eventually she would have to at least give the police the facts. That could wait until tomorrow though. For now she would let the doctors gather their physical evidence. Then, for a short while, she could wrap herself in the security of a clinical white paper gown and immerse her exhausted body and soul in the warmth of a well-trained WPC's caring words with limitless cups of milky coffee.

#

Timeline: Sunday morning 9am

Lynden Brace sat in Cellestra's dressing room, waiting for the police and paramedics to arrive. He did not know how to cope with panic. This unfamiliar disabling emotion seemed to scramble his thought patterns and switch all actions to autopilot. On discovering Cellestra's body he had waited a few hours before calling the emergency services. He had then contacted David Moon to break the sad news. David's phone had immediately switched to voicemail so Lynden's carefully chosen life-changing words had to be left in a recorded message. Now he sat in the tranquillity of Cellestra's dressing room trying to calculate the outcome of the previous evening's events.

The fact that the celebrated Psychic had selfishly over-dosed on a Paracetamol and Cherry Brandy cocktail was not a surprise

111

to Lynden. He congratulated himself on the fact that her accidental suicide had been one of the possible scenarios he had considered; given how 'unhinged the stupid booze swilling bitch was' he thought. However, Millie's successful escape from her kidnapper could bring unwelcome repercussions for the illusionist, and this was a far more difficult situation for Lynden to evaluate. There was also the other small matter of it becoming headline news that Cellestra had bought a winning lottery ticket. That was something he had totally failed to factor in to his wide range of possibilities. Lynden sat on one of the cream sofas in Cellestra's dressing room and took in a deep breath. He ran his hands through his slick black hair before rubbing his tired eyes and letting out a purposeful sigh. 'Why couldn't the silly fat cow stick to the script?' he thought.

Lynden couldn't shake off the uneasy feeling that the impending media storm would focus on Millie's ordeal and his name would be forever associated with such an evil plot. It would be like an unpredictable steamroller thundering down a steep hill; the outcome could be totally out of his control unless he was able to jump into the driver's seat and pull on the brakes. His 'Fooling the Nation' plan had been perfectly executed until Cellestra had unexpectedly bought a winning ticket and attracted unwanted publicity; her daughter's escape had been a second unpredicted event. Lynden knew that there would be a full investigation and he was at risk of being at the centre of a career-killing scandal.

Lynden fully expected that one day in the far off future the full extent of his marvellous deception would leak out. He knew either Cellestra would unwittingly do or say something stupid to impress a chat show host; or that her money-grabbing husband would try to exploit the whole episode to further expand their psychic empire in some way; perhaps boasting of their antics in an autobiographical account of the whole event. In anticipation of this outcome, Lynden's lawyers had been careful to include numerous clauses in the legal documentation that had been drawn up with Brendan Fagg. These protective clauses and conditions would serve to exonerate Lynden of any wrong-doing when the deception of fixing the Shimmer Stakes lottery draw was eventually unearthed. However, Millie Moon was an un-known entity. How would the media react to the teenager's story? Once the insatiable pack of news hounds had got their teeth and claws ripping through the events, would Lynden Brace be painted as the hero who was simply trying to help a family in need? Or was he in grave danger of being cast as a villain who took advantage of the Moon's awful predicament to further his own career?

He tried to take his aching mind off the swirling torrent of scenarios flashing through his brain. Gazing up at the wall, he noticed Cellestra Moon's timeline of newspaper cuttings that lay behind a spotless pane of glass, charting her rapid rise and phenomenal success. His head tilted to one side as he quizzically studied the framed pieces of yellowed newsprint that lay behind the glass. Deep in thought, Lynden rubbed a hand across his face and began to stroke the hairs of his smart purple-black goatee beard.

Lynden Brace had always insisted on methodically checking out the backgrounds of anyone who would be involved in any of his shows. Whether they were a celebrity or a wannabe, he couldn't afford to be sued by anyone who claimed to suffer any long-term psychological affects from his illusions. So, before he created any event for his 'Brace Yourself' series, each and every participant's history was thoroughly investigated. The new Fool The Nation lottery episode was no exception, and Lynden's team had thoroughly researched his subject. He knew every tiny facet of Cellestra Moon's life and career path; so here in the serene silence of the celebrity Medium's dressing room, it was obvious to the trained mentalist that something very important was deliberately missing from her wall of carefully selected memories. Peter Frogson, Millie's biological father, was nowhere in sight.

#

Timeline: Sunday afternoon

Richens and Duke entered the room in the Serious Assault Suite; both giving a cursory nod of 'hello' at the woman constable who had patiently stayed with Millie throughout her

113

sleepless hours. In an almost well-established synchronised movement both detectives sat down on the opposite orange coloured sofa and Duke switched on an audio recorder.

Throughout the afternoon Millie re-lived and re-counted every waking moment from the last seven days; not one detail had been over-looked as each piece of information she had given to the officers was questioned and scrutinised. DI Richens' barraging fire of questions wanted to know why had she gone out that night? Why had she so readily got into that taxi? Why did she think her captors had kept her alive? Exactly how had she managed to escape from the factory? Sergeant Duke noticed the change in his boss's demeanour. He realised Richens was unsure whether to believe Millie really was the victim of a vicious kidnapping. Unknown to Duke the wily inspector's suspicions had been raised when he first heard that Millie had turned up safe and well. Richens had now begun to consider that she could have been part of her parents' elaborate scam to defraud the lottery and dupe the whole country.

"Am I free to go home yet?" asked Millie.

"Yes Miss Moon, you're free to go whenever you want to," replied Duke supportively.

"But there is something I need to show you before you leave," stalled DI Richens with a dry smile.

Richens placed a silver disc into the slot of a DVD player. It clicked and whirred in the drive and the television screen immediately burst into life. An aerial image of the foyer at the TV studios appeared. It gave an uninterrupted view of Cellestra Moon addressing her adoring public. The date recorder in the bottom right hand side of the screen confirmed that it had been filmed just over a week ago on the evening of Cellestra's final show on the 'I Can See You' tour. It looked like any normal meet and greet event. Millie stared blankly at the screen.

"What is this?"' she muttered to herself

"What could there possibly be on this CCTV that is of any interest to me? It's just my fat-arsed over-protective mother pissing about as usual, playing the queen to her adoring fans, doing fuck-all and trying to justify her existence. Where is the selfish old cow anyway?" Richens stared back at her in silence.

114

"She couldn't even stay sober enough to come out and pick me up when I escaped from that hellhole, and she's probably nursing a hangover now rather than acting like a proper mother and coming to get me." Millie took a glug of coffee before sinking down into the sofa to reluctantly watch the video footage.

"I suppose she's swanning about doing some theatrics about how she's managed to cope with me being kidnapped; claiming all the spotlight and fame, when it was me who had to go through that fucking nightmare." The detective noticed the colour suddenly begin to drain from Millie's face, she became subdued; her angry demeanour was gradually replaced with the look of total fear as she continued to stare at the TV. On the screen she could see a red haired woman hand Cellestra Moon a small oblong lavender coloured package which the Medium graciously accepted and handed to David Moon. He then unceremoniously deposited it into the gift collection sack. Immediately the red haired woman turned and left the group of fans. But the way the woman walked was familiar to the scared teenager; the wobbling movement of the stranger's head evoked such terrible memories. The Styrofoam coffee cup slipped from Millie's fingers and bounced onto the tiled floor, splashing hot coffee over her feet. She was oblivious to the scalding liquid seeping through the top of her paper forensic slippers. All she could see was a taunting vision, all she could feel was absolute frozen terror. The chaperoning WPC who had sat quietly in the corner of the room observing the whole interview, immediately rose to her feet.

A burning rage that seemed to grow from a furnace deep within the pit of Millie's stomach was beginning to rise. Her head pounded to the whirring fan of the disc player as an uncontrollable tremor began its unrelenting journey throughout her arms and legs. Clammy beads of sweat were running across her brow as she tried to hold back the torrent of bile now foaming from her mouth. She was powerless to hold back the sickly wave of vomit. The policewoman hastily grabbed a metal waste bin from beneath the table and passed it to Millie. Richens paused the CCTV recording and reached into the inside pocket of his sports jacket to retrieve a packet of disposable paper handkerchiefs. Deftly he took one from the pack and passed it to Millie, before purposefully putting the sticky tab in place to secure the remaining contents of the packet. The WPC opened the office door and asked a passing PC to arrange a glass of water for Millie and something to clean up the coffee spills. Richens walked over to open the office window. He continued to watch Millie silently shiver in the corner of the room as the WPC placed a reassuring arm around the frightened teenager's shoulders.

Moments later the PC returned to the door and softly tapped on the obscured glass windowpane before entering with a tumbler of mineral water and a mop and bucket. Millie raised her feet up off the floor as the PC washed foaming disinfectant over the tiles. He had thoughtfully brought a separate soapy sponge with him that he handed to the WPC who used it to wipe over Millie's feet. A couple of moments later the air was filled with the zing of a pine forest. Millie took a sip of water and wiped the paper handkerchief across her lips. The helpful PC turned to look at DS Duke.

"By the way, I was just on my way to tell you Sarge, there's someone at the front desk with an important message for you and the Inspector," said the PC.

Richens was intrigued by Millie's shocked reaction to the video footage and he began to slowly walk around the office, glancing across at his colleague.

"Go and see what the message is downstairs will you Duchess," he whispered. DS Duke got up from the sofa and left the room with the PC. Richens fixed a steely stare on Millie's face.

"Did you recognise something on the footage?" asked Richens, resuming his position on one of the orange coloured sofas.

"Or someone?" he coaxed. Slowly the patient detective took a deep breath and brought the palms of his hands together, raising his index fingers towards the fine pointed tip of his nose and tucking his thumbs beneath his chin in his trademark prayer pose. The young girl nodded back at him, taking a small sip of water.

116

"Okay, we'll carry on then." Richens flicked the rewind button on the remote control and immediately the woman on the screen bounced back into action. Richens paused the recording, freezing the red haired woman's face on the screen. Millie remained motionless, except for her eyes that switched from staring at the television to staring at the wet floor, then flicking back to the frozen screen. In fact she would look anywhere except at Richens' gaze.

"So Millie, what do you think?" Millie took another sip of water and continued to stare at the tiled floor.

"Come on Millie talk to me." Richens spoke softly. He slowly got up from his sofa and walked over to Millie's side of the room.

"I can't find who did this to you unless you help me. And I want to bring them to justice just as much as you . . . ."

"She's a liar" said Millie, coldly interrupting Richens verbal flow.

"All my fucking life she's pretended to be someone else; pretended that I'm someone else," hissed the teenager, struggling to hold back her pent up fury.

"My dad's not my dad, my real name's not Millie and my twatting waste-of-space mother risked my life just to protect her own made-up fucking reputation." A hot stab of anger punched through Millie's heart.

"Where is the heartless bitch anyway?" she cried.

"Millie, the screen, what can you see on the screen?" pressed Richens, but his words simply washed over her.

During the long, rain-swept journey to the police station, David Moon had reluctantly confirmed that what the kidnappers had told Millie about her mother was the truth. She was the daughter of a feckless scam clairvoyant and a drug dealer. Afterwards, in the detached anonymity of the Serious Assault Suite, Millie had thought long and hard about the circumstances that had led her to endure such a terrifying ordeal. Now, in the pine disinfected concrete office of a cold grey police station, she had begun to accept the realisation that the whole wonderful protected bubble she called her life had all been a well constructed, calculated lie. Her over-bearing mother had not been protecting her; she had instead been looking after her own

117

interests. 'The selfish old mare had always been more concerned about her own wealth and reputation than her daughter's happiness,' thought Millie. The self-absorbed thoughtless Cellestra had even been too drunk to answer the call when Millie had escaped, and it had been David who had come to her rescue. Stinging deep inside with anger and humiliation, Millie continued to stare at the damp tiled floor in stunned silence, as two fat salty tears began to slowly fall down her hot face. Richens reached into his pocket again for his pack of disposable handkerchiefs, and gently handed one to her.

"Come on Millie," said Richens returning to his soft even tone.

"Help us catch the people that did this to you." Millie slowly raised her gaze from the floor, her eyes meeting Richens' steely glare. Pausing to clear her throat she took another sip of water.

"The woman with the red hair in the video, she's just another bitch pretending to be someone she's not," whispered Millie.

"It's not a woman. It's a man," she faltered

"She's one of the men from the factory. The lispy bastard with the knife. I'd know that wobbly-headed fucker anywhere."

There was a soft knock on the door and Richens recognised the familiar outline of the figure through the obscured glass to be DS Duke. Richens walked over to open the door, constantly watching Millie as she shivered and rocked on the sofa in the corner of the room. The WPC placed a comforting hand on her shoulder. Millie tried to listen to the detectives' conversation as they talked in hushed tones in the open doorway. Duke handed his boss a piece of A4 paper, smiled sympathetically at Millie and left the room.

Millie stared coldly at the Inspector. Richens could sense the emotion flooding through her, he could almost feel the pain burning in the pit of her stomach; the sheer eruption of anger about to burst to the surface. But now he was about to unleash a final cruel blow that would severely affect Millie's fragile state.

"Millie," began Richens softly. She gazed back silently.

"I'm afraid I have some terribly tragic news," he was hopelessly searching for the right words to use; the right way to deliver such an unexpected body blow to the trembling teenager. But there was no easy way to launch such a bomb shell.

"Your mother was found dead in her dressing room earlier this morning."

Millie's head buzzed with the overload of information. As she listened to each of Inspector Richens' carefully chosen words she felt an unexpected sting of guilt spread through her veins. Millie remained seated, huddled on the sofa. Slowly she raised her head and silently turned to meet Richens' stare. He beckoned her towards the open door of the room.

"Thank you Millie, that'll be all for now." She stared back at him blankly.

"Thank you Miss Moon," repeated Richens, a little unnerved by Millie's relatively calm reaction.

"You're free to go love," whispered the caring WPC.

Slowly and silently Millie rose from the comfort of the soft orange sofa, her gaze still firmly locked onto Richens as she left the sanctuary of the room. She slowly made her way down the soulless corridor into the waiting protective arms of David Moon.

Chapter 11

Timeline: Monday morning 10am

The stifling hot air in the CID office felt as if every breath of oxygen had been sucked out of it. All of the office windows had been snapped open and numerous electric fans whirred continually in a vain effort to cool the heavy atmosphere. DI Richens was standing in front of the white melamine incident board briefing his team of detectives.

A series of photographs taken at the factory unit where Millie had escaped from were pinned to the wall next to the board. The forensic investigations from the scene had so far shown no conclusive evidence to confirm the kidnappers' identities or their intentions; however the steely detective firmly believed had the teenager not been so resourceful and determined to get out of there, then he could very well have been looking at a murder scene today.

"Right, what do we know about Kyle bastard Cedel?" demanded Richens.

"He's a geek," jeered a voice from the back of the room.

"Yes," agreed Richens, writing down the word beneath Cedel's name on the board.

"He's fond of using aliases to give him a sense of anonymous power," offered another detective from the front of the group.

"Yes, thanks for the amateur profiling lesson," muttered Richens dismissively as he drew an arrow-headed joining line between StarBoy and MagicMan on the screen.

"His middle name isn't bastard sir, as you first suggested." Trudi Jones was standing in the doorway. Richens spun around and stared at her incredulously.

"His middle name is Matthew sir," continued the pretty blonde DC with a smile.

"Okay," accepted Richens, adding 'Kyle M Cedel' to the growing list of clues.

"Any other points of enlightenment coming from Cybercops?" asked Richens sarcastically. Trudi entered the room and perched on the corner of Sergeant Duke's desk.

"Actually yes sir," she continued.

"I've done some digging and found he's got a twin brother called Bryan. The records don't say whether he's an identical twin, but no-one's heard of him for years anyway. They also had another sibling, an older sister, but she died about seventeen years ago." Richens jotted down the name Bryan in small lettering at the edge of the incident board. Pausing slightly he turned back to face Trudi.

"Does Bryan have a middle name too?" he asked sarcastically.

"Yes sir, Neil. His middle name is Neil." Richens made a note of 'N Cedel' after Bryan's name. Trudi turned around on the desk and gave DS Duke a triumphant smile.

"You have been a busy girl haven't you?" whispered Duke with a playful wink.

#

Timeline: Monday evening

Kyle Cedel was fastidiously cleaning his small bed-sit flat. The sticky carpet had been nagging at him for a couple of days now and he could no longer endure the faint aroma of stale cigarettes and beer that clung to the air in this impromptu bolt-hole. How people could lazily live their lives surrounded by such filth was beyond Kyle's comprehension. He had ripped up the worn carpet to reveal the original Victorian oak floorboards that lay beneath. He had then spent most of the day disinfecting every surface in the small square bedroom until there was no hiding space for any dust or any trace of the previous lazy chavvy occupants. Kyle continually checked the time on his watch. 'Nearly seven thirty,' he sang to himself with an excited smile, as he smoothed down the starched cotton duvet cover on his neatly made single bed. News of Cellestra Moon's death had come as a complete surprise to Kyle Cedel. That was something he regarded as an unexpected bonus; something that he felt

121

deserved to be celebrated. The rolling news channel had stayed with the story throughout the past 48 hours. It had bounced from one development to another; from Avani Kapoor announcing Cellestra's accurate prediction of the winning lottery numbers; to the Medium's incoherent outburst outside the stage door, followed by an emotional announcement from a family friend that the country's most adored Medium had passed away. Finally it had been confirmed that early investigations suggested the celebrity Psychic had taken her own life with an accidental overdose of pain killers and alcohol.

Kyle was pleased there had been no mention of Millie Moon's abduction in the news. It appeared that Cellestra had been surprisingly true to her word and had not involved the police. He was happy that the media had made no mention of the turmoil the woman had been in during her final hours; she would receive no additional sympathy from the public.

"I'm glad the fat old cow suffered and no-one knows how much," he mused with a wry smile. Kyle's mobile phone rang loudly, interrupting his thoughts. He peered down to see a familiar number in the display. Much to Kyle's annoyance, his brother had continually called him over the weekend. He had rejected all fourteen calls and ignored all of the impatient text messages. Defiantly he pressed the red button to send yet another call from Bryan Cedel to voicemail.

Since hearing the news of the Medium's death, Kyle had chosen not to answer his accomplice's phone calls. He was lying low for a while and ignoring his brother. He knew Bryan would be angry with him, as calling the celebrity Psychic and forcing her to confess to being a fake hadn't been in the Cedels' original plan. Kyle was embarrassed that he had allowed his emotions to get the better of him, but in his twisted mind he believed that he had been dealt the rougher hand in the deal. Bryan knew his brother hated the filthy environment at the factory unit, yet Kyle had been forced to reluctantly visit their prisoner each day with protein drinks. Given the choice he would have dispensed with Millie in Witches' Wood on the first night, but Bryan had insisted they keep her alive. Kyle's growing resentment towards his brother was beginning to develop into a small rebellion. News reports of Cellestra's correct prediction of the lottery numbers had enraged him. It had initially appeared that the Cedels' plot to bring down Cellestra's empire had backfired and the Medium was momentarily held in even higher esteem by her adoring public. Kyle could not cope with the fact that he had been inadvertently instrumental in bolstering Cellestra's reputation. He had sought to rectify that mistake with a couple of telephone calls to the tabloid press, claiming the Shimmer Stakes lottery had been duped by the Psychic. He had no idea his actions would plunge the Clairvoyant totally over the edge. Now Cellestra was dead, Kyle believed the whole saga had played out better than either he or his brother had planned. Revenge was sweet, his work was done and he no longer had to take any instructions from anyone else; least of all from bossy Bryan.

Kyle hadn't visited the factory unit for a couple of days. As far as he was concerned Millie was still safely imprisoned there and she could die from starvation for all he cared. He was blissfully unaware that Millie had escaped.

The defiant young man sat on the edge of his single bed and slowly leaned down to check a small leather holster strapped to his right ankle. Inside was a newly sharpened hunting knife. He decided that he would return to the factory unit to attend to his captive prey later on that evening. But for now he had other plans. A broad smile grew across Kyle Cedel's pale white face. He had accomplished his long held mission; he had helped to bring about the demise of Cellestra Moon, and tonight he was going to celebrate. Kyle's self-indulgent thoughts were interrupted by a soft knocking on the door of his bed-sit. He stood up from the bed and hastily smoothed down the edge of the duvet cover before opening the door to greet his visitor.

The woman standing in the doorway was more attractive than any of the others Kyle had met through Sci-Fi-Dater before. The website was Kyle Cedel's particular online dating agency of choice. It was frequented by other disenchanted sci-fi loving singletons looking for relationships. Its domain name used a clumsy play on words that appealed to the less imaginative geek. The woman that MagicMan knew as The Magician's Assistant was living up to every beautiful pixel of her profile photograph, and Kyle immediately knew that one way or another, their evening would conclude together; whether she was willing or not.

The small framed woman had startling green eyes that were strangely familiar to him. Her friendly smile greeted him warmly as he beckoned her through the doorway and into his scrubbed bed-sitting room. She wore a stylish black leather jacket and skinny black jeans. Her glossy chestnut coloured hair was styled in an efficiently cut bob that just brushed above her shoulders. She was carrying a screw-top bottle of wine in one hand and she clutched a couple of science fiction DVDs and the handle of a shiny black and silver rucksack in the other.

"Hello," said Kyle, nervously. The pale skin on his face began to blotch with colour.

"You must be my Magic Man?" purred the beautiful woman, walking confidently into the room.

"And I hope you're my Magician's Assistant?" replied Kyle coyly, the pitch of his voice rising at the end with a slight drying of his mouth. She noticed his head twitched nervously from side to side when he spoke.

"Yes, but as I told you in the chat room, my friends call me Rose," she continued. Her shiny chestnut bob caught a glint of light coming from a bright orange floor lamp that was positioned by the window. She placed the wine and DVDs on a small desk in the corner of the room and casually hung her black and silver rucksack on the back of a chair, before slowly unzipping her leather jacket. Kyle caught a breath of her heady perfume as she took a step closer to him. Her green eyes flashed around the room before returning to meet Kyle's awestruck stare.

"Have we met before?" asked the nervous young man. He was sure there was something familiar about her but he couldn't quite place it.

"In your dreams maybe?" replied Rose playfully. Suddenly the intrusive trill of Kyle's mobile phone pierced the air one more time.

"Don't you need to answer that?" asked Rose after the fourth ring.

"No," replied a mesmerised Kyle, casually switching off the phone and placing it on the desk.

124

"It's only my brother, it won't be anything important," he added dismissively. The young man spoke with a lisp and he hated the way he found it difficult to pronounce his Rs correctly. Following many hours practising speech therapy exercises Kyle had managed to largely overcome his flaw, however he still had the occasional slip, especially when he was nervous or excited.

Rose peeled off her leather jacket to reveal a figure hugging T-shirt beneath. It was a classic fantasy film vest top that featured a faded image of a muscular futuristic warrior brandishing a light sabre. Kyle was speechless, his gaze firmly fixed on Rose's pert breasts that lifted and fell beneath the vintage garment. Rose sat down on the edge of the single bed, slightly crumpling the freshly laundered linen. She looked around the room quizzically, as if searching for something. Kyle stood by the doorway, almost paralysed with the anticipation of how he planned the evening would end.

"Do you have any glasses we can pour that into?" asked Rose, pointing at the bottle of wine on the desk.

"Yes, of course," he smiled, hastily licking his rasping tongue over his dry lips to try and moisten his arid mouth. Kyle opened the door of a small pine cupboard that hung on the wall next to the TV. He took two freshly washed coffee mugs from the neatly stacked bottom shelf and passed them over to Rose. His body began to tremble slightly as her fingers brushed lightly over his hands; his dry top lip stuck to his top row of uneven teeth. Her vibrant green eyes flashed up at him as she took the mugs from his grasp.

"I hope you like Rosé," whispered Rose.

"It's my favourite wine," she cooed as she unscrewed the cap and began to pour the pink frothy bubbles into the two coffee mugs.

"Wosé for a wose," mewed Kyle as he eagerly drank down the sparkling liquid that instantly refreshed his parched mouth. Damn it, his speech impediment had returned. Rose smiled warmly as she re-filled his coffee mug with more of the pink frothy bubbles.

'My perfect woman,' he thought, as a nervous smile grew across his thin gingery lips. Kyle had decided that tonight was

125

going to be MagicMan's reward for a job well done. Cellestra Moon was dead and he would soon be celebrating between his freshly laundered sheets, with his more than willing Magician's Assistant, and nothing was going to interrupt it.

#

During the two days following Cellestra's death, Kyle had ignored all calls and texts from his brother. When Bryan Cedel had visited the industrial estate he was greeted by a blockade of blue flashing lights. The entrance gates to the compound were heavily guarded and access to the factory unit was totally out of bounds; it had obviously being identified as a crime scene. Bryan had at first been irritated by the unexpected and sudden cut in communication from Kyle. When he overheard a police officer say that a young kidnapped girl had escaped from the factory, Bryan's initial annoyance with his sibling had become totally engulfed by fear and then rage. The Cedels' Nemesis may be dead, but her petulant teenage daughter could now become a liability. A constant stab of fear stung through Bryan's heart; maybe Millie would be able to identify her kidnappers. Bryan knew his brother could be careless when he was excited or nervous. He worried that Kyle may have given the girl clues about her captors and left incriminating forensic evidence at the scene. He was well aware that Kyle had many twisted perversions and he remembered seeing him behave strangely around her on more than one occasion. It had always been his sadistic sibling's intention to kill the girl once they had witnessed Cellestra's downfall, so Kyle may not have been too bothered about Millie seeing his face. In Bryan's mind it would only be a matter of time before the frightened teenager was able to give the police crucial information that would lead them to the twin brothers' door. He needed a new plan to cope with the aftermath and he was incensed that Kyle had chosen such a critical time in the operation to ignore him.

Bryan parked his car in the road opposite the building where Kyle lived and tried to call him one more time. He had seen his brother's visitor arrive and enter the apartment block half an hour earlier. Bryan had recognised the young woman instantly.

126

Despite her transformation into an alluring red-headed temptress, he knew her as the formerly plump journalist Rosie Carmichael.

"Come on, come on, pick up the damn phone for God's sake," he muttered. After the first ring Kyle's mobile clicked to voicemail but Bryan hung up again without leaving a message.

"What the fuck are you playing at you cretin? Don't make me come up there and fucking sort you out," he rasped, slamming his phone down onto the front passenger seat. He hastily searched in his jacket pocket for an asthma inhaler as a creeping paranoia began to fester through his brain. As he took a large lung-expanding gasp from the inhaler, Bryan began to imagine his brother's choice to ignore his calls could be something far more sinister than a self-indulgent act of defiance. And what was that journalist doing there? Had Kyle double-crossed him, gone to the papers and come to an arrangement for his side of the story?

'Kyle, you're such a fucking unreliable squealer,' thought Bryan. What if his brother had struck a deal with the authorities? After all, being an ex-con, Kyle had more to lose than Bryan if the pair were found guilty of the kidnap plot; but implicating his squeaky clean twin sibling as the main perpetrator could mean a lighter sentence for the ex-internet troll. Bryan remained in the car and patiently waited for his brother's red-headed visitor to leave.

#

Timeline: Late Monday night

DI Richens' gaze was still firmly fixed on the white melamine incident board. He mumbled to himself as he recounted every facet in the case so far. DS Duke watched wearily from the opposite side of his desk. Three other detectives working on the case were busily scribbling down notes from Richens' briefing. It had been another very long day and Duke was missing out on the promise of a take-away curry and bottle of wine on the sofa with Trudi Jones.

"So, the main central character to all of this is the late Cellestra Moon, AKA Carol Frogson." said Richens, circling her name on the incident board with a fat blue marker pen. He was updating the board with some additional information about Cellestra's background that the grieving David Moon had eventually given to him.

"Not forgetting of course, her daughter Emily, AKA Millie, who was kidnapped, which kick-started this whole investigation." DS Duke had now decided to simply nod his head at thirty second intervals whilst taking the opportunity to close his eyes momentarily, as his boss repeated his observations for the third time.

"The kidnapper, who we strongly suspect is Kyle Cedel, has a trolling history and a strong fixation with proving that Cellestra Moon wasn't genuinely psychic," continued Richens.

"So having failed in all previous attempts to expose her as a fake and bring her down, matey boy comes up with this kidnap plan to extort the ever-so-popular Ms Moon into submission," he continued wearily. Duke simply watched as his boss took a different coloured marker pen and began to draw connecting red lines all over the incident board; as if joining the names together would solve the case, like joining the dots in one of his brainteaser puzzles.

"So then," he coughed, bringing Duke out of his micro-nap with a startled twitch.

"Cellestra's ever-so-supportive husband, David Moon knew that the game would be up unless they could convince the kidnapper that his wife could come up with the goods. So he suggests bringing in the slippery Lynden Brace. His job is to pull off the illusion that she's successfully predicted the winning numbers. Is that right Duke?" Richens turned towards his Sergeant searching for affirmation; yet looked accusingly at his colleague like a school master quizzing an errant schoolboy.

"Err yes, slippery Brace sir," nodded a weary Duke in agreement.

"Right then," announced Richens, returning his gaze to the melamine incident board.

"So where did it all go pear shaped?" he asked rhetorically; not expecting anyone sat in front of him to have a remote clue

128

as to where his train of thought was leading. The small team of assembled officers looked at each other in the vain hope that one of them would offer some assistance to Richens' rambling presentation.

"I reckon the fly in the ointment was when the TV news channel announced to the world that Cellestra Moon had apparently predicted the correct numbers. That's the problem right there," asserted Richens as if his Sergeant fully understood his moment of realisation.

"Don't you see?" he asked incredulously. DS Duke nodded in unconscious agreement whilst looking blankly at his boss.

"The kidnapper gets pissed off 'cos the whole scam has only served to boost Cellestra Moon's reputation. Cedel is on the back foot Duchess 'cos he thinks she's going to wallow in all the glory for predicting the numbers accurately; she's even got an independent witness from the newsagent's shop who will verify her psychic ability. So that totally screws up the kidnapper's plans to reveal Ms Moon as a fake." DS Duke sat up in his seat in an effort to feign his understanding of his boss's sudden late night epiphany.

"So, to wreak his revenge, Kyle Cedel contacted the papers and the local news channels to give them enough ammunition to suggest lottery fraud, which fired them up to go round to the studios to quiz Cellestra about her winning ticket. She then crumbled under the pressure and topped herself with a Paracetamol and Brandy cocktail. He bloody well pushed her right over the edge didn't he sir?" added Duke, as he rubbed his tired itching eyes whilst trying to stifle a yawn.

"Yes, a kind of death by proxy," agreed Richens. He slowly took a deep breath and ran his left hand across his bristled chin, before bringing his fingers to rest over his mouth beneath the fine pointed tip of his nose. Deep in thought he continued to breathe in and out heavily and stare at the incident board; one hand across his mouth and chin, the other hand aimlessly tapping the red marker pen against his right leg. He knew they were still no closer to tracking down the perpetrator.

"How about taking another look at what Millie Moon had said about her kidnappers?" suggested Duke trying break the encompassing silence by offering another perspective.

Millie had described her captors in great detail. They were almost identical in build, both were softly spoken. The one had wielded a knife and spoke with a lisp. He had sounded more menacing than the other and had a peculiar wobble of his head when he walked. She suspected the second kidnapper was asthmatic. He was a smoker and was often breathless. He had a slightly more prominent gait when he moved, almost like a camp skip. Richens made more notes on the incident board.

"Similarities in their build suggest they could be brothers," continued Duke.

"Exactly. Kyle Cedel has got a twin brother, Bryan," nodded Richens in agreement.

"Rosie Carmichael identified the voice on the radio show as StarBoy, who we know is Kyle Cedel, and Cellestra Moon identified the same voice as being one of the kidnappers on the phone," added Duke.

"Do we have any more on a possible address for Kyle Cedel yet?" asked Richens.

"Well I asked DC Jones to work on that and at one point we thought there was a possible link to a block of bed-sits in Baker's Road, but it was a bit of a long shot as it's a well-known junkies' paradise and the informant is a bit well, unreliable to say the least," replied Duke reluctantly. Suddenly both men became aware of hurried footsteps in the corridor outside.

"Forensics have found a fingerprint and DNA match from a sandwich wrapper and coffee cup found in a bin at the factory in Blackwater Lane," interrupted a babbling PC who had eagerly run upstairs to personally deliver the breaking news to CID.

"And it's a positive match to what we have on record for Kyle Cedel," he wheezed, trying to catch his breath. Richens felt a sudden surge of excitement sting through his veins, as if his heart was about to pound out of his chest. This was the ultimate break he had been waiting for.

Another detective in the office swiftly stood up from his desk. He was on the phone and frantically trying to attract Richens' attention.

"Sir! The kidnapper's mobile has been switched back on sir. We've triangulated the signal it's coming from a building in Baker's Road." Richens smiled across at Duke.

"Come on Duchess, get your coat," shouted Richens excitedly.

"We've got a kidnapping troll to catch."

#

Rosie Carmichael hastily fumbled with a bunch of keys at the front door to her flat. Her trembling fingers shook uncontrollably as she fought to jab the key into the lock. She desperately needed something to take the edge off her hyper-agitated tremor. Thankfully she knew her dealer would be there at any moment to ease the pain.

She slipped inside her apartment and flicked on the light switch. The lounge was simply and tastefully decorated with magnolia coloured walls and a dark oak laminate floor. A stylish long red leather sofa hugged the one wall; a large red half-circle rug lay in front. At the side was a limed-oak coffee table with a large Venetian vase on top. In the corner of the room was a matching desk with a chair beneath. Rosie took in a deep comforting breath as she was relieved to have at last reached the sanctuary of her own home.

Tracking down Casey AKA MagicMan to his low-life little bed-sit had given her a tremendous boost of confidence; finally confronting the horrible little man who had been instrumental in her downfall had been the adrenalin kick of a lifetime. Now, her work was done; sweet revenge had indeed been served. She walked over to the desk and hung her heavy black and silver rucksack on the back of the chair. An abrupt knock on the front door pulled her sharply from her thoughts. It had been a good day and now, with the help of her visitor's bag of tricks, she would be able to relax, unwind and reflect on the evening's accomplishment. Rosie eagerly opened the door to let her dealer in.

#

Richens stared out of the open car window, carefully observing every movement from within the building across the other side of Baker's Road. The dawn sun had disappeared behind a thick blanket of cloud as large heavy drops of rainwater danced on the windscreen. Richens and Duke had assembled a small yet enthusiastic team to carry out an early morning raid on the rather austere looking building. Unfortunately, at that moment, all they had was the building number for the location of where the mobile phone signal was coming from. They had no way of knowing which of the twelve rooms was rented out to Kyle Cedel.

Dusty nicotine-stained curtains hung loosely at most of the windows. A pale amber glow danced in one of the rooms on the top floor where someone had left an orange coloured lamp on all night. Many of the transient occupants of 332 Baker's Road were still sleeping; they would not rise until opening time at the benefits office or methadone clinic.

"He could be hiding behind any one of those filthy panes of glass," muttered Richens as he wound up his car window.

Richens knew it would be highly impractical to just force his way in and arrest everyone in the building; he just didn't have the manpower. He had to smoke out his prey somehow. He opened his car door and stepped out into the lashing rain. Duke followed his boss's lead and soon both men were darting through the torrent of water, their jackets pulled up over their heads in a futile attempt to keep dry.

They arrived at the black imposing front door of the building. A broken intercom panel had been crudely fixed together with brown packaging tape around the edges; a temporary repair that looked as if it had weathered at least two winters. Each of the twelve separate steamed-up panels had a button and a space alongside covered in a plastic shield. None of the residents had filled in their name tags beneath; such was their desire to remain anonymous.

'A palace of broken souls,' thought Richens as he turned the large tarnished central door handle. There was a heavy click and the front door slowly swung open in the breeze.

"Security not exactly a high priority here then," said Duke, quickly peering inside the dank communal hallway.

The building had once being a proud Victorian villa; the home of a successful flour miller. It had been converted into bed-sits in the 1970s and, at first glance, it appeared to the two detectives that no further property maintenance had been carried out since that time. The entrance hall had a parquet wooden floor that had been neglected for so many years that the varnish now resembled the colour of dark treacle. Three dented and chipped wooden doors, that bore the scars of many drunken rages and fits of temper, led off the passageway to the first few ground floor flats. Another door at the end of the passageway led into the tired and dated shared kitchen and then onto the only bathroom at the rear of the house. A narrow dark treacle coloured staircase climbed from the hall up to the first floor landing. Duke flicked the light switch a couple of times before realising there was no bulb in the brittle yellowed plastic fitting that swung high above their heads. The air hung heavily in Richens nostrils as he took in a deep breath of what smelled like a heady concoction of urine and damp dog. A couple of bluebottle flies buzzed hastily past Richens' ears as he followed them up the dark staircase.

Pausing half way up the flight of stairs, Richens took his mobile phone and a small piece of paper out of his inside breast pocket. He began to punch in the numbers that were neatly written on the notepaper in front of him. Duke looked at him quizzically. Slowly Richens raised his forefinger to his lips to indicate he required silence. Suddenly somewhere in the distance they could here the trill of an unanswered mobile phone.

Slowly, Richens made his way up the second half of the treacle coloured staircase. After six rings the kidnapper's phone automatically clicked to voicemail. Richens stopped midway on the second flight of stairs and ended the call. He paused momentarily before smiling back at Duke and pressing the redial key. Again the ringing started. This time it was getting louder as the two men made their way along the darkened second floor landing towards the door that led into room number nine.

Richens' hand-picked team of armed officers had entered the building and now silently tip-toed behind him; like a long black snake of body armour and bullet-proof helmets. The ringing stopped again. Apart from the persistent buzzing of a couple of flies, the whole house lay silent. Even the torrential summer rain outside could not be heard deep within this dank chamber of lost souls. Richens paused once more before redialling the pay-as-you-go mobile phone number.

Richens and Duke stood quietly outside the dark brown chipped wooden door of room number nine. There was a pale strip of light around the whole badly fitted door frame. It was coming from inside the room and partly illuminated the dank corridor outside. The two detectives could see no sign of movement in the light; there were no shadows to break the continuous line of pale brightness around the door. Again Richens pressed his redial key. A ringing phone chirped loudly behind the door in front of them. After six rings it stopped and Richens' call was again diverted to voicemail. Calmly Richens softly knocked on the door.

"Mr Cedel it's the police. Please come to the door," he asked politely. There was no reply. The only sound was the continual hum of the two jostling bluebottle flies that seemed to be persistently exploring the crack of light around the doorframe, trying desperately to find their own way into room nine. Richens placed his hand on the door handle, drew in a deep breath and turned his hand slowly to try the latch. The door's Yale lock had secured it shut.

Richens stepped aside from the door and indicated to one of the armed officers to use his metal battering ram to force their entry into Kyle Cedel's single bed-sit. After one swift blow to the flimsy wooden door lock they were in. Two shouting armed officers entered the room as Richens and Duke watched a shower of wooden splinters cascade into the dusty air.

Kyle Cedel lay face down on top of the starched duvet that covered the single bed; his slightly built white body was motionless. He was wearing a pair of pale blue coloured Y-fronts; the label clearly on show, as it awkwardly poked out of the top of the waistband. His face was buried in a soft feather pillow with just a mop of ginger hair visible from the doorway.

His right arm was bent at the elbow with his hand slid beneath the pillow to support his head. Kyle's left arm dangled limply off the mattress; his fingertips having taken on a slight purple pink colour. The two bluebottle flies joined the rest of an insect army that jostled around Kyle Cedel's lifeless body.

DI Richens looked around the room. A slight odour of stale perfume hung in the air but, in contrast to the rest of the building, the bed-sit was unexpectedly clean and tidy, clinical even. There were no curtains hanging at the sparkly clean windows and the frames and window sill appeared to have been scrubbed clean with pine disinfectant. A small desk had been placed in front of the window which had a wallet, two mobile phones and a couple of unopened sci-fi DVDs on top of it, along with a leather ankle holster that contained a small hunting knife. In the corner of the room an orange coloured floor lamp shone brightly.

On the one wall was a small plasma TV screen next to a pine cupboard. Opposite hung an over-sized sci-fi film poster featuring a muscular futuristic warrior holding a light sabre. Duke commented how that size of poster was a true vintage collector's item, as it would originally have been used in cinemas to promote the film when it was first released.

"Who'd have thought a piece of paper from 1977 could be worth so much," snorted Richens, secretly proud that he had managed to impress his colleague by casually mentioning that he was aware of when the first film came out.

Deftly, Richens took a biro from his inside pocket and used it to prise open the door of the small pine cupboard on the wall. On the bottom shelf were four coffee mugs that featured sci-fi film characters, their handles all neatly facing in the same outwards direction. Above were a couple of tins of baked beans, an unopened loaf of bread and a tube of biscuits. The items all uniformly positioned with their labels on show.

"A bit of a neat freak," commented Duke.

"Yes," agreed Richens.

"But look at this," Richens pointed at the bottom shelf of the cupboard. Duke stared blankly back at his boss.

"I can't see anything out of place sir," said Duke, slightly perplexed.

135

"Well the thing is Duchess. This neat freak, as you like to call him, was just a little bit more OCD than most." Duke still looked on confused.

"I think there are a couple of coffee mugs missing from this shelf," said Richens triumphantly pointing at an empty space alongside the mugs.

"I can't see any other mugs hanging around in the room," he added. Duke shrugged his shoulders, unsure where his boss's observation was leading.

"Well, someone this obsessive about their surroundings would have been driven made by four coffee mugs on the left and a big unfilled asymmetrical space on the right."

"Maybe he only had four mugs sir," offered Duke.

"No!" asserted Richens.

"If he only had four mugs then believe me they would have been placed in the centre of the shelf, or spaced evenly." Duke looked at him curiously.

"Wow how could you possibly know that?" he asked in awe of such perception. Richens smiled as he pulled out his phone.

"Ah Duchess, it's just an old obsessive family trait of mine," he whispered with a smile.

"Let's get SOCO up here and find out what killed him. But I bet if we find those missing mugs, they'll lead us to the answer."

Chapter 12

Timeline: One week later –
Monday mid morning

Millie Moon stared out through the black tinted windows of the stretched limousine. The crowd gathered in the church yard had steadily grown all day. A row of reporters jabbed microphones into the sea of sad faces behind them; repetitively firing questions, asking how the fans felt at the sudden and unexpected death of the country's most adored Medium. Behind the blacked out windows of the car Millie anonymously studied the sympathetic faces on the line of people along the driveway. Cameramen unceremoniously clambered over the old gravestones to gain a better vantage point of the funeral cortege; tombstones of a bygone era had become impromptu leaning posts for a wide collection of tripods and shiny silver flight cases. The continual whirl of video cameras and cross-fire questions unceremoniously captured every reaction from the waiting crowd of mourners. Flashing and whirring throughout the day, the cameras had mercilessly documented every emotion as TV reporters gave their pieces to camera. Everyone's patience was now being rewarded with a front row view of the arrival of Cellestra's hearse and the grieving entourage.

The limousine drew up outside the large gothic wooden doors of the church. Millie turned towards David Moon; he gave a small reassuring smile. There was a collective gasp from the gathered crowd of fans, celebrities and well-wishers, as they watched Millie emerge from the car. Any spark of petulance had been totally extinguished from this once fiery teenager. Millie stared at the cobblestone pathway in front of her, avoiding any eye contact with the hoards of reporters flocked around the entrance. She tightly clutched David Moon's arm and began to walk slowly yet purposefully from the car towards the large heavy wooden church doors.

DI Richens and DS Duke stood quietly at the rear of the church, carefully observing the black-clothed sea of mourners in front of them. The officers quickly ascertained the only members of Cellestra Moon's family in the congregation were her ashen-faced daughter Millie and grieving husband David. The rest of the assembled flock were celebrities and TV personalities who had been carefully invited by the studios; a strategic move on their part to gain every possible column inch of press coverage available. From pop stars, TV chefs and weather girls to soap stars, chat show hosts and news anchormen; Brendan Fagg had ensured that anyone who was anyone at the TV studio was in attendance, and any new up-coming stars he needed to promote had been given seats in direct sight of the cameras. Cellestra Moon may have been dead but her funeral show was one cash cow he was going to milk for as long as it was humanly possible.

Avani Kapoor was seated on the pew behind Millie Moon. Richens and Duke recognised her as the girl from the newsagents who had benefitted so generously from Cellestra Moon's accurate lottery prediction. Avani gave Millie and David a small smile and nodded her head graciously, as Cellestra's only family members turned to take their seats on the row in front of her.

David Moon shifted uneasily on the hard wooden pew as he watched his wife's coffin slowly pass by his tear-filled eyes. The six well-choreographed pallbearers lowered the white and gold coffin onto its plinth with metronomic precision. There it stood; a large pearlescent flower-bedecked casket that held the mortal remains of the country's most adored Medium.

David Moon reached into the inside breast pocket of his jacket and slowly pulled out his wallet. A neatly folded paper handkerchief lay in the fold. David removed the handkerchief and used it to dab away a salty tear. He gazed back down at his open wallet and saw a small photograph of his late wife smiling up at him. He grinned back broadly. He knew that tucked away behind that heart-warming image of Cellestra's smiling face lay a winning lottery ticket. No one was ever going to spill the beans thought David deviously; 'no one will ever know that I was one of the other three people that bought a winning ticket' he smirked to himself, as he quickly slipped his wallet back into his jacket pocket.

The TV Company had already begun to rake in a fortune off the back of the merciless posthumous marketing of Cellestra Moon. Like all artists, the country's most adored Medium was now worth so much more to them dead; far more than she ever had been worth when she was alive. Fortunately Cellestra's reputation had escaped relatively unscathed following her brandy-fuelled rant at reporters. Lynden had somehow managed to pull her away from the ravenous pack of newshounds just before she had given a full confession of her misdemeanours. Her drunken tirade was blamed on mental exhaustion; that in turn led to her untimely death. The claims from an anonymous tip-off to the press that Cellestra was a fraud and had duped the Shimmer Stakes lottery were simply dismissed as untrue. Brendan Fagg had already lined up a future series planned around contact with the dead Medium, and they were just searching for the right star to head up their new show. There had even been tentative suggestions behind the scenes that Millie Moon should take the mantle.

All of the limited crew that had been involved in the filming of the sham lottery show had been given such large bonus payments and lucrative career promises they would never dream of opening their mouths; the highly suggestible audience had been convinced they had taken part in the live draw. Brendan Fagg had also given Lynden Brace his own twelve-show series and agreed that the illusionist could have a totally free creative reign.

Cellestra's demise had become the hotly debated subject of many late-night chat shows that week, with hundreds of claims made by hoards of conspiracy theorists. They firmly believed that the celebrity clairvoyant had accurately predicted the lottery numbers and had then been immediately silenced by powerful mysterious forces. Her growing army of believers simply refused to accept the official cause of her accidental death; an overdose of painkillers and alcohol.

David Moon smiled inwardly as he ran over the financial facts in his calculating mind. He could cash in his winning lottery ticket and no one would ever be able to object to it being

139

a fix. He would still receive the royalties from all of the existing film rights, DVD and book deals documenting Cellestra's life; and now the growing conspiracy theorists would serve to germinate yet another revenue stream from the cash cow that David had created.

No one was about to let the cat out of the bag that Shimmer Stakes' lottery ticket buying public had been swindled. After all, the public had a totally unconnected innocent winner of a quarter of the lottery jackpot in Avani Kapoor. The studio had announced that the proceeds of the winning lottery ticket Cellestra had bought would be donated to charity. David Moon's smile grew wider as he decided he would cash in his winning ticket as soon as the coast was clear. After all, he would be able to retain his anonymity for as long as he wished and no one ever needed to know.

Millie couldn't help but notice how her step-father's demeanour had changed. He had replaced his wallet in his inside jacket pocket, and was now looking almost gleeful as he stared at Cellestra's coffin and lightly tapped his chest. He had begun to nervously click his right heel on the flagstone floor and continually checked his watch. From the back of the seated congregation Richens thought the grieving husband looked almost impatient, as the Vicar began to deliver his opening speech of the service.

At the end of the second hymn, Lynden Brace rose to his feet and walked towards the lectern next to where Cellestra's casket lay. He gazed at the floral tributes that covered the lid of the coffin and took in a deep contemplative breath; the mixed scent of lilies and white roses reached his nostrils. Quietly and reverently Lynden prepared to deliver his eulogy. He unfolded a crisp piece of A4 paper in his hands. He smiled inwardly as he looked at the rows of neatly printed, carefully chosen words on the paper in front of him; words that Lynden Brace planned to use to help the gathered masses come to terms with the loss of their psychic friend.

"I am sure many of you sitting in this church today were at some point touched by Cellestra Moon," he began.

"Indeed many hundreds, if not thousands gathered outside or watching this service on television today, will have all, at some

140

point, felt touched by Cellestra Moon." Lynden studied the front row of sad faces sat before him.

"Her generosity of spirit," he continued, looking squarely at Avani Kapoor and then to David.

"Her hard work and drive to build up her empire." Brendan Fagg looked down at the floor trying to avoid Lynden's steely stare.

"And finally, her love for her family," his eyes met Millie's tear-filled gaze.

"But I don't remember Cellestra for any of those fine qualities," announced Lynden. The almost catatonic congregation suddenly shifted uncomfortably in their seats.

"Cellestra Moon was not my friend; we were not family either; I can't say we even knew each other all that well," he continued almost dismissively.

David Moon's heal suddenly stopped tapping, his smile evaporated. He stared directly at Lynden. What was the cool, calm and collected showman about to reveal?

"So why would I accept the invitation from Cellestra's family to stand here in front of you all today, to talk about the country's most adored Medium; someone that I hardly knew?" A fine bead of sweat ran down the side of Brendan Fagg's hot round face. David's leg began to twitch nervously.

Richens and Duke watched two reporters on the back row begin scribbling frantically in their notebooks. A couple of mourners tried to stifle their coughs. Everyone on the front row appeared to be anticipating they were about to hear an unwelcome revelation from the master illusionist. Could Lynden Brace be about to reveal the TV studio's darkest secret? Could he be so cruel to sully the memory of the country's most adored Medium at her own funeral? Was he really that desperate for the publicity? David Moon shuffled uneasily in his seat as he prepared to stand. But Millie placed a reassuring hand on her father's arm, pulling him back down, as they both turned to look accusingly along the row at Brendan Fagg.

Lynden took in another deep breath, a classic dramatic pause that he used in many of his stage shows to build tension in the audience. The calming floral scent from the bouquet on top of Cellestra's coffin soothed his nostrils as he raised his hand to his forehead. He smiled at the congregation and tapped the side of his head, as if subconsciously pulling the words he needed from his brain. He then slid his closed hand back down the side of his face, running his fingers through to the point of his smart purple-black goatee beard.

"Let me tell you something," blurted Lynden at last, appearing to go off script.

"This is something I'm pretty sure none of you will know. Cellestra Moon influenced my life in such a way that it helped me to become the person I am today." The uncomfortably tense atmosphere inside the church eased slightly.

"I know, it's incredible but even I could see that Cellestra had a special gift. She was someone who gave so many people hope when they felt hopeless; comfort at a time when they felt inconsolable. She helped the bereaved to believe that they were not alone, and she always gave them enough encouragement to . . ." Lynden paused as if his carefully crafted manuscript in front of him no longer contained the right words.

". . . find the courage to move on," he said, faltering as he swallowed hard and blinked back a tear. Brendan Fagg breathed out a long sigh of relief. The TV executive was almost overwhelmed by the generous endorsement given by the mentalist; thanks to Lynden's recognition of the Medium's abilities, many sceptics would be temporarily silenced and the studio would be able to continue milking their psychic cash cow for many years to come. Lynden's carefully written eulogy continued, as he highlighted the recent years of Cellestra's successful career; he then thanked the studios for their unwavering support of such an unconventional field of entertainment, before drawing his tribute to a reassuring close.

"And now Cellestra, as you take your final journey to the other shore; your faithful followers will put on their rose tinted glasses for the last time and we'll all look up to the heavens." Lynden paused once more, observing how most of the congregation had now dutifully lifted their heads to look at the ceiling above.

"Those whose lives you touched here on this mortal earth," he continued with a smile.

"We will never forget you Cellestra Moon. We'll never forget the things you did."

Lynden delivered his unscripted address with such genuinely heart-felt passion that the whipped up congregation felt poised on the edges of their seats; coiled and ready to jump to a standing ovation at a second's notice.

"So, as we bid a fond farewell to the country's most adored Medium, we'll all try to remember," the showman gazed up at the roof and smiled again.

"The spirits are always calling." His last few words delivered with a heavy Mancunian accent in tribute to the late Lancashire lass.

The people gathered inside the church rose to their feet, a small flurry of claps trickled through the pews. Outside the crowds began to cheer in appreciation as a wave of applause whooshed through the open wooden doors and enveloped the whole of the building. Lynden made his way back down the aisle towards his seat. Celebrities and wannabes blew kisses; those standing by the aisle vied to place a hearty congratulatory slap on his back. He had gained the trust and respect of Cellestra's followers and his heart-rending performance would be covered by national TV and every newspaper in the land; his work was done. The congregation remained standing to sing another hymn. Lynden folded the crisp piece of A4 paper into four before carefully tucking it inside his waistcoat pocket.

Richens and Duke remained standing at the back of the church as they watched the last of the mourners follow Cellestra's coffin out into the graveyard.

"Well that service certainly had its moments," sighed Duke. Deep in thought, Richens simply nodded and smiled back at his Sergeant. Slowly he took a deep breath and rubbed his hands over his face, bringing the palms of his hands together and raising his index fingers towards the fine pointed tip of his nose; the trademark prayer pose that Richens always adopted when deep in thought.

"Someone's missing though Duchess," he said, quite self assuredly.

"Who sir?" asked Duke.

"That junkie-bint Rosie Carmichael, that's who Duchess." DS Duke looked quizzically at his boss.

"Maybe she couldn't get on the guest list sir, I mean have you seen how many celebrities there are here today?" suggested Duke.

"That's as maybe, but she's a resourceful type of bird. I reckon she's got enough contacts to wrangle an invitation. She'd definitely want to be here today to see for herself that Cellestra Moon was dead and buried; no way on earth would she want to miss that."

\#

Lynden didn't attend Cellestra's burial after the service; he believed that should be a private moment attended by the family and close friends only. The funeral cortege had journeyed to the farthest side of the cemetery where a small wooden cross and mound of freshly dug earth awaited the arrival of the country's most adored Medium.

Lynden had patiently waited for half an hour until the last gaggle of reporters and well-wishers had been ushered down the driveway of the churchyard, before he took a stroll between the old grave stones. Casually he leaned against the reassuringly sturdy trunk of an oak tree and took a silver cigarette case from his left jacket pocket. He removed one of the pre-rolled herbal cigarettes from the case and raised it to his lips. He snapped the case shut and put it back in his pocket before searching aimlessly in his trouser pockets for a light. Suddenly his fingers found the familiar outline of a book of matches. His mood was instantly lifted as he knew he could now indulge in a quiet moment's contemplation with the heady herbal aromas filling his lungs.

"Hello Lynden," whispered a soft voice from behind the tree. Lynden continued to smoke his cigarette. He drew deeply on the rolled-up herbs and quietly blew the smoke back over the hot glowing tip to re-ignite the embers. Slowly he turned around.

"Hello Millie," he replied with a small hint of surprise in his voice. The blonde teenager smiled back at him. Lynden noticed

144

she looked more mature than her eighteen years. She was wearing a smart tailored black skirt suit with a crisp white camisole blouse beneath. She wore her hair tucked up inside a shallow brimmed black hat. He noticed she was trying hard to avoid losing her balance, as her very high black patent leather stiletto heels kept sinking into the soft grass beneath her feet.

"I just wanted to thank you for . . ." she paused.

". . . well for everything really."

"There's no need to thank me Millie," said Lynden reassuringly.

"No, honestly, there is," she replied.

"My Dad, err David . . . "she faltered, swallowing hard.

"David Moon told me how you tried to help; all the great things you did for my mother and me. I just wanted to thank you personally." Millie reached out to shake Lynden's hand.

"And your eulogy today was extremely touching . . . so generous," she cried.

"Where is your Dad?" asked Lynden, trying to deflect some of the young woman's sorrow.

"I have no Dad," replied Millie with a cold shrug of her shoulders. Lynden looked at her quizzically.

"Oh, you mean where's that money-grabbing bastard David Moon?" sneered Millie.

Startled by Millie's small outburst, Lynden put his arm around her shaking shoulders and walked her over towards a nearby wooden bench. The trembling teenager shivered with each tear as she told Lynden that David Moon had stood at her mother's graveside and proudly confided in her that he had bought one of the winning lottery tickets. Millie's rage was plain to see as she revealed David was planning to cash in the ticket and use the money to help launch her career. She was to take the place of Cellestra as the next generation of most adored Medium.

"David said that it would be even easier to pass me off as a Psychic . . . far easier than it had been with my mother, as her fans would believe that her gift had been handed down to me somehow," she snivelled.

"He's always got his eyes on the fucking prize. How the hell could he even bring up such an idea at my own mother's funeral?" Lynden hugged the now sobbing teenager into his chest and took another deep draw on his herbal cigarette.

"It's just too soon Lynden, too raw. How could he even think that I'd be okay with any of that?"

He took his silver case from his jacket pocket, clicked it open and offered it to Millie. She shook her head.

"My mother doesn't like me smoking," said Millie.

"Ah but these are herbal ones, not tobacco," soothed Lynden.

"I can't cope with ordinary cigarettes because of my Asthma," confided the mentalist.

"Any way, it might calm your nerves and I don't think your mother's about to complain is she?" he asked, wondering if the small joke was totally misplaced. Comforted by his kindness and the man's ability to make her smile at such a sad time, Millie took a small roll-up from the case and lit it from the glowing end of the almost burnt out embers of Lynden's cigarette.

"I'm just so sick of it all," cried Millie as she took a long drag on the spidery joint.

"You know, all the time I was in that horrible factory unit I had a lot of time to think about my life Lynden." He smiled back at her.

"Funny how thinking you're going to die can give you a totally different perspective on things."

"Like what Millie?" asked Lynden, nonchalantly stubbing his cigarette out on the flagstone path.

"Oh I don't know. It's just before it all happened I was perfectly happy to waste my life going out, having fun, being a general pain in the arse to my mum," Millie laughed.

"But now . . . well maybe now I need to grow up a little and be a bit more responsible. Who knows? Maybe David's right." Lynden looked back at her quizzically.

"Maybe I should do something constructive with my life. But it will be on my own terms, not to David sodding Moon's schedule." Millie took another couple of long, slow draws of her cigarette and looked up defiantly towards the sky."

146

"See Mother! I'm perfectly capable of making my own decisions, look I'm even managing to smoke a herbal spliff all by myself," she giggled.

Lynden and Millie remained huddled together on the wooden bench looking out across the graveyard and fields beyond, as the young teenager's mood began to mellow with each drag on the joint.

"Thank you so much for today though Lynden, your eulogy was just what Cellestra's fans needed to hear," she whispered.

"Maybe in time I will carry on where my mother left off," mused Millie with a sleepy sigh.

"What harm can it do eh?"

Lynden lit another cigarette before placing the slim book of matches into his waistcoat pocket. He took great care not to disturb the piece of folded paper that contained the words he had carefully chosen for Cellestra's eulogy, as that innocuous sheet of vellum now lay alongside an older piece of faded lavender notepaper that was wrapped around a small dried flower – a Poppy.

#

Timeline: Monday afternoon

Richens and Duke sat opposite each other in the CID office. They had just returned from Cellestra Moon's funeral and Duke was taking a short break, staring blankly at Richens' unfinished crossword. His boss was deep in thought; eyes closed with his elbows leaning on the metal desk, Richens' hands were held in a prayer pose just beneath the pointed tip of his nose.

Cellestra Moon had been buried; the prime suspect in her daughter's kidnapping now lay in the mortuary; his cold remains awaiting formal identification as Kyle Cedel. Although the case felt as if it was drawing to a close, Richens still had an uneasy feeling. He hated loose ends and Rosie Carmichael was a loose end. Just like a loose thread on a jumper, Richens hated the thought of a small snag of doubt. In his mind he knew they had a habit of quickly unravelling into a full blown failure of a

147

case. He couldn't close this investigation until he had spoken to Rosie one more time.

Richens also had the nagging question of what had happened to Kyle Cedel's partner in crime. No clues had come back from the dead body discovered in Witches' Wood. He was an as yet unidentified male with no previous criminal record. The taxi had been stolen from the Crucible Cars' garage earlier on the day of the kidnapping. Millie had been positive that both of her masked captors were men; slightly-built and effeminate but definitely men. One had an awkward gait when he skipped about in the darkness. The kidnappers had mostly talked in whispered tones which had made it difficult for her to distinguish their voices or accents clearly. Except for the one time when the more menacing kidnapper with the lisp had slid the blade of his knife over her flesh; that day the other man had shouted forcibly across the factory unit, but still she could not pick up on any accent. But they had definitely been male voices.

Despite Millie's insistence that her kidnappers were both men, the highly instinctive detective still had his uneasy feeling that some things in her descriptions could also point to one of the captors being a woman; slightly-built, effeminate, skipping gait. Had Rosie Carmichael been Kyle Cedel's accomplice? Had she dropped off the mobile phone at Cellestra's meet and greet in the foyer?

DS Duke sat opposite his almost meditational boss and flipped his newspaper over to look at the solutions to the crossword that had so far eluded him. Richens opened his eyes and noticed the answers had been printed upside-down at the bottom of the page. Suddenly his mind flashed back to the evening when Rosie Carmichael had been in their office. He noticed the Manila case folders on his desk and remembered Rosie's vacantly staring reaction. Had she been able to read the names StarBoy or MagicMan circled at the top? If she had worked in newspapers and printing rooms all of her life then she would be used to reading text upside down. Richens took a deep breath as he slowly came to the stomach churning realisation that he had probably given Rosie Carmichael the scoop of her life.

"You fucking idiot!" scolded Richens.

"Who?" asked Duke, startled by his Inspector's sudden outburst.

"Not you Duchess. Me," he replied as he pulled his laptop screen into view.

"Cedel died from a drugs overdose didn't he?" Duke quickly folded away the newspaper and sat up straight in his seat, a puzzled look on his face at the unexpected remark.

"That bint Carmichael had something to do with it, I'm sure of it. Maybe she read one of Kyle Cedel's aliases written on the tops of the folders," added Richens. The sergeant was finding it difficult to keep up to speed with his boss's racing thought pattern.

"It's a long shot I know," continued Richens, his mind frantically searching for an answer.

"What if she did an internet search for StarBoy or MagicMan, added Cellestra Moon's name into the mix and that gave her enough of a spark to track him down on other sites. Who knows maybe she got lucky, joined the right forums and managed to strike up some sort of weird online friendship with him. I wouldn't put anything past that devious junkie bitch," hissed the annoyed Inspector.

Richens began frantically clicking through documents on his PC searching for the results of Kyle Cedel's toxicology report. He scanned a long list of files on the index, opened up one called NO-ID2-09-2015-TOX. The laptop whirred into action as the document opened up on the screen. It stated that the male awaiting formal identification as Kyle Cedel had died as a result of heart failure brought on by a heroin overdose.

"Ah ha, I knew it," said Richens triumphantly.

"There was nothing on Kyle Cedel's prison file about him being a smack head when he was inside was there?" conceded Duke, slowly getting up to speed.

"No. Nothing. There was no tourniquet around his arm or other track marks on the body when we found him either. So, I reckon someone killed him Duchess and tried to make it look like he took his own life." Suddenly Duke heard a soft ping sound come from his own laptop to indicate he had a new email message.

"If that's Cyber Cop asking you out on another date then tell her you'll be lucky if you get home before Christmas at this rate," sniped Richens, almost jealous that Trudi Jones had officially become Duke's new girlfriend.

"No it's SOCO's report from Baker's Road sir," replied Duke hurriedly.

Duke quickly clicked opened the message as Richens walked around the desk to look at the screen. The report stated the scene of crime officers had carried out a thorough search of Kyle Cedel's bed-sit, the communal areas and the alleyways at the side and rear of number 332 Baker's Road. One of the mobile phones found in the bed-sit had been used to send the ransom messages in the Millie Moon kidnapping. The last five incoming calls had been from DI Richens' mobile. Two other numbers in the phone's call history were to the handset given to Cellestra Moon at the TV studios, and the Medium's personal mobile number that had been called shortly before her death. There was a third outgoing phone number that had been contacted only once. This call had been made immediately after the last time the phone had been switched back on. The owner of that mystery number still hadn't been traced.

On the second phone found in the flat there were nineteen missed calls in the log but no voicemail messages had been left. Half a dozen text messages from the same anonymous pay-as-you-go phone all demanded Kyle to call back. It was plain to see the tone of each message had become increasing urgent. SOCO were still trying to trace the owner of the phone that had called more than a dozen times leading up to the death of Kyle Cedel.

The SOCO team had also found an empty wine bottle and two smashed coffee mugs just inside the top of one of the communal wheelie bins half way down Baker's Road. Richens had asked the forensics team to look out for the items, and the mugs they found matched the set of four that were neatly stacked inside the cupboard in Kyle Cedel's flat. The broken crockery had traces of wine and Rohypnol on them, which matched the contents of the nearly empty bottle of Rosé found with them.

"Looks like forensics also pulled a good set of prints off the mugs and bottle in the bin," said Duke, quickly scanning the document.

"Hmmm, Kyle Cedel's and Rosie Carmichael's," murmured Richens peering over Duke's shoulder.

"And Rosie's prints are on one of Cedel's phones too."

"So it wouldn't be too far fetched to assume his killer is Rosie Carmichael. As I said she managed to track him down somehow and then wormed her way into his bed-sit. What do you reckon Duchess? She takes a pre-loaded bottle of wine with her and knocks him out with the Rohypnol first. Then the junkie bitch pumps his arm full of enough of that Heroin shit to wipe out an elephant?" Richens stood up from his perch on the corner of Duke's desk and walked over to the incident board.

"So, Kyle M Cedel . . ." continued Richens circling the name on the melamine board.

". . . was murdered by Rosie Carmichael. She must have been his accomplice in the kidnapping," he concluded with a flourish of his pen around Rosie's name.

"Right Duchess, let's get a warrant organised, that smack head journo is not going to be able to wriggle out of this one. Casey Kyle Cedel ruined her life did he? My arse he did. They were in this together all along."

Richens stood back triumphantly from the board. He was about to wipe off all the other multi-coloured connections his marker pens had previously made, when something suddenly caught his hawk-like stare. Slowly he tapped the end of his black felt pen against his bottom row of front teeth.

"You bastard!" he exclaimed.

"Gotcha!" a broad smile creeping across his thin face.

"Come and see this," beckoned Richens to his sergeant.

Duke was putting on his jacket in anticipation of the impending trip to Rosie Carmichael's address. He couldn't quite see what had caught his DI's attention or what could possibly be more important than arresting Rosie for the abduction of Millie Moon and the murder of Kyle Cedel. To him the incident board resembled a plate of multi-coloured spaghetti with spasmodically placed photographs and names of victims, suspects and other people loosely associated with the case dotted around the edges.

"Look here," demanded Richens.

"The letters in the name Lynden Brace . . ." he paused.

". . . it's an anagram . . . a bloody anagram of Bryan N Cedel."

Duke looked on in bewildered astonishment how his crossword-loving boss had managed to fathom out the connection.

"Ah, I see. Just like KC became Casey, the purple twin-set's alter ego couldn't quite break all his ties with his real life could he sir?" confirmed Duke.

"Nah, just like a fuckin' psycho nutter, he couldn't help himself, always got to leave a clue in there somewhere. But I had a feeling there was something too good to be true about that slippery bastard. Twins are even worse with their 'special connection' crap," snorted Richens, as he raised his hands to mime a set of inverted commas.

"The pair of them must have been plotting their evil plan for years. Duchess, you go over to Dozy Rosie's place now. I need to go and pay the Moons' chief mourner a little visit," announced Richens as both detectives swiftly left the office.

Chapter 13

Timeline: Monday evening

The drive over to Cellestra's wake had given DI Richens enough time to re-wind and re-play the facts of the case several times; cold hard facts that were hard to deny. Cellestra Moon had undoubtedly been a fake. Her daughter had been kidnapped by someone who had absolute faith in their knowledge that Cellestra Moon was a fake. The police had traced the kidnapper's phone to the bed-sit of an internet troll who now lay dead. Millie had escaped from the kidnappers and she was adamant that her captors were all men. It was unclear exactly how this chain of events would unravel, but Richens was sure there was another player here, another puppet master that had been pulling all of the strings; someone whose name was an anagram of Bryan N Cedel perhaps? He was certain that could only be Lynden Brace.

Richens allowed a small sliver of doubt to crawl through his mind. Could the man who had been so instrumental in helping the Moon family during their ordeal, possibly turn out to be the twin brother of a dead kidnapper? The twin brother of an obsessed man; a mad man who had plotted throughout his whole adult life to bring the celebrity clairvoyant down? The two men shared some physical similarities and, just because they were twins, it didn't mean they had to be identical psychopaths. They were both slightly built, but Lynden Brace's physique appeared to be more toned than Kyle Cedel's pudgy body. Kyle's hair was wispy and ginger whereas Lynden Brace had always proudly displayed a head of thick dark purple-black hair.

"Damn it!" muttered Richens.

"It's fucking hair dye and possibly a syrup; of course. Lynden Brace dyes his hair or might even wear a wig," a broad smile grew across the Inspector's leathery face. He continued to run through the other facts in his mind.

"Surely Millie would have recognised Lynden's voice if he had been one of the kidnappers though?" Another doubt flickered through the seasoned detective's mind.

The terrified teenager had described the first kidnapper's voice as having a pronounced lisp; a sinister tone which matched the recording of Kyle Cedel speaking on the phone in radio show. The second captor had been a heavy smoker and had spoken with a wheezy cough. Both voices were very different from Lynden Brace's flamboyant tones. Could the anagram of Lynden's name simply be a coincidence?

At the end of a tree lined service road, an ornately hand-crafted wooden sign had been securely screwed to a set of wrought iron entrance gates. It indicated that DI Richens had arrived at 'Moonbeams,' the Moons' family home. Cellestra had chosen the artisan sign herself from a vast collection displayed on a local artist's website. In contrast to the clean lines of the star's dressing room, she had always preferred to feather her semi-rural retreat with objects of a rustic style. The understated hand carved nameplate was the least pretentious of an otherwise ostentatious selection available from the studio's catalogue.

The Moons' house was a modern, wooden clad detached building set back off the quiet country lane. Its design had suffered badly at the hands of a conceptual architect who had failed miserably to deliver his promise of an idyllic alpine chalet in suburbia. He had instead presented the family with a building that resembled an over-grown garden shed which quickly became the butt of many a local neighbourhood joke.

Richens swung his car through the open gates, coming to a slow stop on the block paved driveway. He flashed his ID at an usher standing on duty by the front door and made his way into the large open dining hall.

David Moon was standing at the bottom of a very wide marble staircase, chatting to a small group of celebrities. Richens recognised the entourage as a group of teenage boys that had recently won the latest TV talent series of Band Warz. They were a rap-band collectively known as Waguan Da Hood and they had pulled the magic green lever on the Shimmer Stakes' lottery show the week before. The four young rappers looked uncomfortable in their matching designer black suits.

They all swayed unsteadily as they drank their third flute of champagne in what they disrespectfully referred to as 'the freaky dead momma's crib.'

David noticed Richens out of the corner of his eye and immediately made his way towards the front door to greet him.

"Inspector Richens," announced David as he warmly held out his hand.

"Mr Moon," replied Richens nonchalantly, his eyes scanning the group of people in the hall.

"I didn't know it was usual for the police to come to the wake?" enquired David tentatively. Richens continued to search the room, his gaze darting from face to face.

"I need to speak to Lynden Brace please," announced Richens with a hint of panic in his voice. David looked back blankly.

"I haven't seen Lynden since the service in the church," replied David.

"He didn't come to the burial and I don't think he came back here."

One of the Waguan Da Hood rappers had overheard the conversation and slowly swaggered over to Richens.

"Ooh you mean the mind bending dude," said the teenager, swaying in front of the detective.

"Whooo," he continued, wiggling his fingers over his head as if to mock the illusionist's ability.

"Have you seen Lynden Brace since the church service?" asked Richens impatiently. Another member of Waguan Da Hood joined his friend in front of the officer.

"Nah man, me and me bloods ain't seen him innit; not since we saw he'd hooked up with the bootylicious Millie dudette in the death yard." Richens stared back at the delinquent stood before him as he mentally translated the statement into plain English.

"So you saw him with Miss Moon in the graveyard after the funeral service? So where is Millie now?" He shot a look over at David. David shrugged his shoulders.

"Err, actually I don't know," he answered sheepishly.

"We had bit of a row just after we buried her mother and she stormed off to cool down. I guessed she'd got a lift back with someone else."

"You damn fool," replied Richens.

"What is wrong with you people? After all that poor kid has been through and you just let her wander off. Wasn't one kidnapping enough for you?" David stood in stunned silence as the Inspector's words ricocheted around the marble walls. Richens turned away from the shocked entourage and walked quickly towards the door, hastily grabbing his mobile phone out of his pocket. Once back in the private haven of his car Richens called Duke's mobile phone. On the fourth ring Duke answered.

"Err, hello sir," his Sergeant sounded a little flustered.

"Duchess, the mind bender has gone AWOL and I think he's taken Mini Moon with him," said Richens flatly.

"I need every unit out there to search for Brace's car. Are you at Dozy Rosie's gaff yet?"

Duke was standing in the middle of the lounge in Rosie Carmichael's apartment. The room was very brightly lit with numerous halogen down lighters recessed into the ceiling. The detective's gaze was fixed on the broken Venetian vase that lay shattered on the dark wooden laminate floor at his feet. It was the only sign that there had been a struggle within the flat. An answer phone machine blinked in the corner of the room on top of the limed-oak desk. Hanging loosely from the chair beneath was Rosie's black and silver rucksack that still contained Kyle Cedel's laptop computer.

The lifeless body of Rosie Carmichael lay spread-eagled beneath the archway that separated the open-plan living room from the kitchen. She lay face-down on the hard wooden laminate floor. Duke noticed her black skinny jeans were still buckled up at the waist, the bottoms tucked inside her calf length boots; her vintage vest top lay unruffled around her slim torso. Rosie's sharply cut bobbed hair lay limply at her shoulders, covering a cluster of black and purple bruises on her delicate neck.

"Yes sir, I'm here" said Duke.

"But I'm afraid Rosie Carmichael is dead sir. It looks like she's been strangled."

Richens asked Duke to meet him back at the station. He hung up the phone as a shock of fear crawled through his weary body. His mind began to race through endless questions. Where was the one place that Lynden Brace would feel safe? Where no one would think of looking for him? Where the hell was Millie Moon?

Chapter 14

Millie opened her heavy sleepy eyelids. She awoke in the front passenger seat of Lynden Brace's classic sports car; her body enveloped in the warm comforting aroma of leather hide bucket seats. Slowly she began to focus her eyes on the unfamiliar surroundings as she turned her head and blinked at Lynden.

"Hello sleepy head," he said, concentrating on the road ahead.

"Did you have a nice little nap Millie?" Confused, Millie looked at him quizzically.

"Where are we?" she asked with a small yawn.

"Don't you remember?" replied Lynden.

"Wow I guess that small joint must have really knocked you out," he added, still concentrating on the road ahead.

"You argued with your dad . . . err David and we agreed that you needed somewhere to spend the night," he offered reassuringly.

"Somewhere safe." The car began to slow down.

"And here we are," announced Lynden as he pulled on the handbrake with a swift jerk.

The hot summer sun had set behind the horizon. Millie felt a cool breeze flow over her exhausted body as Lynden opened her car door. Still a little disorientated from her sleep, Millie felt weak as she groggily got out of the car and stepped onto the path in front of a modest end-of-terrace house. She held on tightly to Lynden's arm as he led her through the front garden. They made their way down a narrow paved pathway that meandered through waist-high yellow straw-like grass, edged with scratchy rose buses. Numerous thorns dragged into the soft flesh of Millie's legs as she clung onto Lynden's guiding arm, until they arrived at a panelled front door. The front door had once been bright white, but over the years the plastic had been aged by the sun and it now appeared to be brittle and yellowed.

Once inside, Millie's nostrils became filled with the damp and musty air that filled every inch of the oppressive interior. Lynden flicked a switch and the room was suddenly illuminated by four wall uplighters that were equally spaced around the room. Heavy floral pink and green curtains hung at the bay window; they were framed by a large pleated pelmet and swags and tails of green material edged with pink lace. The curtains had once been held back with two pink plaited tie-backs; but these had now been unclipped and the heavy tasselled cords hung freely at each side of the window dressing. Lynden pulled a matching heavily tasselled cord on the left hand side of the bay window and the curtains drew together, meeting uniformly in the middle.

Millie felt as if she had entered a nineties time capsule. The living room walls had been covered in woodchip wallpaper and split horizontally by a dado rail. The top half of the wall above the dado rail had been painted in Aquamarine, the bottom half in Terracotta coloured paint. A green chintzy sofa and two matching chairs filled the space along one wall. They were neatly positioned in sight of a large deep television set that was built-in to a dark wooden corner cabinet. An old dust-covered video recorder perched on the shelf underneath. Next to the cabinet was a matching dark wooden sideboard with leaded glass doors, behind which lay an assortment of sherry decanters, vintage bottles of spirits, wine glasses and tumblers.

A large cast iron gas fire sat inside the adjacent brick-built fireplace. On the mantelpiece was a varied collection of dusty family photographs. A flame haired woman with a tall dark-haired man held a small baby in her arms. There was another photograph, older and a little faded, of two freckly ginger-haired twin boys standing behind an older red haired girl sitting on a swing.

Millie sat down at one end of the chintzy sofa. She kicked off her stilettos and sank her feet into the dusky pink sculptured carpet.

"What is this place," she asked Lynden who was searching inside the sideboard for a decent bottle of wine.

"Oh it's a bolthole that's been in my family for years," he replied casually, reaching to the back of the cupboard for a dusty bottle of Burgundy.

"Don't worry though Millie, you're quite safe here," he smiled reassuringly as he pulled two tumblers from the shelf and uncorked the bottle of vintage red wine.

Millie thought it was a little odd for him to say that she was safe; it hadn't crossed the young woman's mind that she had been in any danger today. Lynden poured out the wine and passed one of the cut-glass tumblers to Millie.

"I hope you like Burgundy. It's all I can find I'm afraid."

Millie sipped the heavy red liquid. She noticed it cling to the sides of the glass like syrup, as she swirled the tumbler in her hand.

"What did you mean I am safe?" she asked.

"That's the second time you've said that today. I didn't think I was in any danger anymore?" Lynden sat down beside her on the floral sofa. He locked his steely gaze onto Millie's pale blue eyes.

"I didn't want to mention it before, but I can't help wondering what David Moon is up to," he said, slyly planting his seed of doubt in the teenager's mind.

"Who knows? Maybe he planned the whole kidnap thing just to get the lottery money for himself; maybe the kidnappers are still out there looking for you." Millie's whole body tensed, like a scared rabbit caught in the headlights of Lynden Brace's steely glare. She took another comforting sip of Burgundy wine.

"I know the police said they'd found their main suspect," he continued.

"But that poor dead man could have been just one member of a much bigger gang. Didn't you say there were two or three men who kidnapped you? They were probably watching the church today, the studios and your mum's house even."

Millie stared back into Lynden's hypnotic eyes. She knew what he was saying made perfect sense; she knew that she could not rest until both of her kidnappers had been apprehended. 'What if Lynden Brace's suggestion was true?' She thought to herself. 'What if David Moon had actually planned the whole thing?'

Millie suddenly felt very alone in the world, as she realised she no longer had the warm protective arms of her mother to run to; Cellestra's over-bearing control, that Millie had resented

160

so vehemently, was now gone. It had been replaced with a dark void of fear and loneliness that nothing could fill. Millie put down her glass, edged along the sofa towards Lynden and rested her head on his chest. The sad grieving teenager began to sob uncontrollably. Lynden felt slightly awkward as he began to pat her softly on the back. He was not used to such displays of emotion. It was a luxury he had never afforded himself. There was no room for sadness, fear or anger in his neat orderly world. Everything in his life was calculated and measured to the very last degree; he had no room for unpredictable emotions.

During his younger life, Lynden had witnessed first-hand the emotional turmoil of losing a loved one. He had feared he would never be able to cope with the haunting ache in his heart; the guilt he felt after his older sister had been in such a state of utter despair that it had led her to take her own life. Lynden had been unable to save her from the charlatans who had filled her head with messages of hope from the dead; the preying swarm of psychics and clairvoyants who had all served to convince Phillipa Harrison that she could end her torment and be reunited with her dead husband and baby girl. The scared little boy and his sad little twin brother had both felt the hot sting of pain reeling through their veins, as the memories returned to haunt them on every birthday, every Christmas, and every anniversary without their beloved big sister who they always affectionately called Poppy.

Lynden had coped with the loss of his sister the only way he knew how. He could not afford to allow his emotions to cloud his judgement, so he buried them so deep within his soul that they would never see the light of day again. He made a conscious effort to switch off all feelings; the sadness, the fear, the loneliness. He would never suffer the same suicidal fate as Poppy. Instead he would take comfort in the fact that one day her death would be avenged; he would be instrumental in the downfall of the self-proclaimed psychic that had driven his sister to her death. Carol Frogson would be made to pay dearly for her wicked scam.

Bryan Cedel had watched his twin brother Kyle crumble beneath the heavy burden of grief after losing his big sister. Unlike his brother, Bryan vowed, on the day of Poppy's funeral that he would always remain in complete control of every possible outcome, of any possible scenario that his life may encounter. Consequentially in later life the man who would become the consummate mentalist Lynden Brace, had always avoided relationships. Other people's sadness, love, guilt and happiness could be even more unpredictable than his own, so he had never allowed himself to get close to anyone who may have an influence on his orderly world.

Lynden gently stroked the back of Millie's head. Her long blonde tresses swished around her small shoulders. This was not one of the scenarios he had planned when standing in the graveyard back at the church earlier that day. The idea that Cellestra Moon's daughter would be looking to him for guidance through her impending quagmire of depression was an unexpected turn of events. Gently he ran his fingers through Millie's hair and gave her a reassuring pat on the back. He pulled her closer to him and gave her a soft kiss on the top of her head. Millie smiled as she nuzzled into his chest. She once again felt safe.

"It'll be okay," he whispered softly.

"I know what it feels like to lose a mother," he murmured, breathing in the innocent scent of her perfume. Millie opened her eyes.

"When did you lose your mom Lynden?" she asked.

"Seventeen years ago," he replied nonchalantly.

"Well she was my older sister really, but she was more like a mother to us."

"Us?" asked Millie.

"Do you have any other brothers and sisters then?"

It could have been the effect of the old syrupy Burgundy wine, it could have been the warmth he felt from cradling the hopeless Millie in his arms, but in that one unguarded moment Lynden Brace had unwittingly opened the floodgates to the buried chasm deep within his soul.

His mind flashed back through a catalogue of taunting cruel memories; thoughts of how he and his twin brother had suffered at the hands of merciless school bullies. From the very first time they had walked through the school gates the two boys had been an easy target. They were picked on for being ginger-haired;

they received constant jibes about their pale freckled skin and how they couldn't spend too long out in the sunshine. His brother had a pronounced speech impediment and neither of the two slightly-built boys had been particularly athletic. Bryan had been asthmatic, so they had always avoided the rough and tumble of the school football pitch and instead chose to spend school lunchtimes in the library or music room. The bullies spread malicious lies that the two sensitive young boys were freaks of nature and they had been born as hermaphrodites. That was when the cruel nickname of 'the Twingers' was invented; the taunting sing-song jeers that would haunt them in every playground.

"Twingers, twingers, ginger twin mingers. They used to be girls but now they're just swingers."

That nasty Twingers tag had stuck with the brothers throughout most of their junior school years. Bryan and Kyle Cedel had only been able to break free of its grip when their family unit had been blown apart and the two boys had gone to separate schools.

Throughout their tormented school years Bryan and Kyle felt their older sister Phillipa was the only one who had understood their plight; Poppy was the only one who had really cared. Suddenly the memories of that fateful day when he had discovered his sister's lifeless body flooded through Lynden's brain; images of the lavender coloured suicide note flashed before his eyes unleashing every piece of pent-up anger and sadness he had tried so hard to stifle for so many years. He could feel a burning tsunami of pain wash away his layers of carefully buried emotions. Now they were bubbling up to the surface of his calm and collected demeanour; like an out of control magma chamber about to erupt.

Millie felt Lynden's body tense up, as he took in a deep breath and reached for his silver cigarette case.

"I'm just going out in the back garden for a smoke," said Lynden.

"You stay here and try to get some rest."

163

Chapter 15

Richens and Duke were frantically searching through a stack of manila cardboard folders. Photographs, maps, pieces of paper were all strewn across the cold metal surface of Richens' desk. They were looking for any shred of evidence to back up the Inspector's new theory that the elusive Lynden Brace was Kyle Cedel's twin brother.

"Didn't Cyber Cop say something about the Cedels having a sister?" muttered Richens as he burst open another cardboard wallet. Duke immediately picked up his phone to call Trudi Jones. After a couple of rings the officer answered.

"Hi," said Duke softly responding to Trudi's voice.

"Do you remember you found some information for me about the internet troll Kyle Cedel having a brother?"

"Yes Dukey, I remember, he had a twin brother called Bryan I think," replied Trudi. Duke's heart fluttered slightly on hearing Trudi's new term of endearment.

"Well, you also mentioned they had a sister who had died. Do you know who she was? When she died?"

"Err, let me take a look," said Trudi. Duke could hear her fingers tapping the keys on a computer keyboard in the background.

"I'm sure I put it in the file somewhere," she murmured, continually tapping the keys and clicking her mouse.

"Yes!" she exclaimed triumphantly.

"Take a look in the file I emailed to you called CEDEL-K-09-2015-BKGRND. From what I remember they had a particularly dedicated social worker when they were kids. The twins were her first proper case and she was very thorough, so she uploaded loads of notes about them. The folder's got all the family background stuff in it from her." Duke smiled proudly as he thought that his new girlfriend wasn't just an exceptionally pretty face after all. DI Richens and DS Duke closely studied the print outs of Trudi Jones' dossier on Kyle Cedel.

The twin brothers had been born in 1985. Their parents were Phillip and Margaret Cedel, a musician and a lounge singer. The couple had divorced soon after their twins were born. With their father absent, Maggie Cedel had been unable to cope on her own with two new-born babies; so her ten-year-old daughter Phillipa had regularly helped her mother. Phillipa took on the daily tasks of feeding and bathing her little brothers whilst her mother went out at night to sing in pubs and clubs. When the boys were five years old Maggie discovered that her estranged husband had committed suicide, so she would no longer receive any maintenance payments from him. She took her family on a budget trip to Spain for a fresh start; to re-build her career and try to find work as a singer called Maggie Ce. There Maggie Cedel had met and fallen in love with a Spanish hotel waiter called Juan. She had quickly decided that Spain would offer her a better new life, and she promptly moved her family into Juan's small apartment in the centre of Benalmádena. But the passion of the holiday romance soon faded. The fiery Latin temperament of Maggie's new lover soon spilled over and he quickly began to resent his ready-made family. He began to regularly beat the two young boys. When Phillipa had told her mother how the twins were suffering at the hands of Juan, Maggie coldly chose not to believe her children's cries for help. The woman had felt the wrath of Juan's fists herself many times, but she was besotted with her Spanish lover and callously dismissed her children's accusations. She chose to believe that her daughter was jealous that she had found love and was now making a name for herself on the Costa's singing circuit. Maggie claimed the twins had been egged on by their older sister and were simply seeking attention.

When Phillipa turned seventeen she grabbed the first opportunity she had to return to England. Six months later Maggie Cedel's battered and abused body had been discovered washed up on a beach in the Costa del Sol. Juan was convicted of her manslaughter. Bryan and Kyle returned to England and Phillipa was granted formal custody of her two six-year-old brothers.

The young siblings had a relatively peaceful life following the deadly end to their Spanish adventure and Phillipa had raised the boys as if they were her own sons. A few years later Phillipa had married Graham Harrison. They moved into a modest three bedroom semi-detached house at the end of a small neat terrace in Dooley Croft. A year later Phillipa gave birth to their baby daughter Abigail; her very own bundle of joy. Bryan and Kyle had happily embraced their new responsibilities as young uncles; doting on their baby niece at every given opportunity.

However, the Cedel brothers' idyllic home lives were once more sent spinning into turmoil with the news that Phillipa had been involved in a fatal car crash. Her husband and baby daughter were dead and the young grieving mother was left feeling utterly devastated. It seemed the family's bond was once more being tested. The twins tried to support Phillipa. They consoled her, listened to her and tried to help her come to terms with the dreadful fallout from the accident. The two thirteen-year-old boys had believed Phillipa had started to turn the corner; she had begun to understand that she needed to try and get her life back on track. They had no idea what would greet them on that tragic day, when they returned home from school.

Bryan and Kyle had arrived at their sister's house much later than usual that evening, having hidden in the school toilets to try and avoid another beating from the school bullies. The twins had been accidentally locked inside the school and the caretaker had only heard their frantic cries when doing his final rounds for the evening. But the Cedels' tormentors were waiting for them outside the school gates and the twins were chased home by the gang of bullies again. The brothers had no idea that their ordeal would be nothing compared with the absolute horror that lay behind the white panelled front door of their modest semi-detached home. When they had stumbled through the hall, nursing cut lips, dirty knees and torn school uniforms, they discovered their loving, beautiful sister Poppy had taken her own life.

Following the tragic death of their sister, Bryan and Kyle Cedel had been taken into the care of the local council before being swiftly fostered out to two separate families. The house in Dooley Croft was boarded-up, awaiting the outcome of probate that would see Bryan, the elder of the Cedel twins, eventually inherit the family home.

166

Sergeant Duke searched through the faded evidence photos that had been taken at the scene of Phillipa Harrison's suicide.

"Hey, look at this sir," he turned around a photograph of Phillipa's final hand-written note to give his boss a clearer view.

"The colour of the notepaper used for the suicide note; it's the same type as Millie Moon's kidnapper's ransom note."

DI Richens closed the cardboard manila folder that had the filename CEDEL-K-09-2015-BKGRND printed across the top in broad red lettering. He looked across at DS Duke. A cold shudder fluttered down his spine.

"Every one a bleeding heart," muttered Richens, as he jotted down the address of the modest semi-detached house in a quiet Manchester suburb that had once been Bryan and Kyle's childhood home.

"It's got to be the other Cedel brother, hasn't it sir," questioned Duke as he got up to follow his boss out of the office.

"Yes, definitely Duchess. It's either him, or Phillipa Harrison has come back from the dead to reap her revenge on Carol Frogson for driving her to take her own life," said Richens as he reached for his car keys.

"And get your skates on, it'll take a couple of hours to get there," he added, almost pushing his colleague out through the door.

Chapter 16

Lynden returned to the living room. He perched on the edge of the sofa and reached into his trouser pocket for his book of matches to light his last herbal cigarette. Lynden sighed heavily. He was feeling unusually on-edge; a most unfamiliar feeling for the mentalist, and now he couldn't remember where he had placed his matches. He stood up, walked over to the dresser and began to rummage through one of its drawers. Eventually a small smile returned to Lyden's lips as his fingers discovered the familiar plastic outline of an old cigarette lighter.

Millie opened her eyes and sat up on the settee. Suddenly she drew in a fearful small gasp of air as she watched Lynden's lighter spark into life. It was a mauve and gold coloured piece of merchandising that had been handed out to crew members who had worked on Lynden's 'Brace Yourself' series. The motif printed on the lighter featured a gold coloured top hat with some black writing beneath. The memory of where Millie had seen a lighter like that before came flooding back.

She watched Lynden breath out little circles of smoke, but all she could see flashing before her eyes was the asthmatic masked kidnapper who had blown circles of smoke over her in the back seat of the car. She gazed at one of the up-lighters on the living room wall, but all she could see in her mind's eye was the headlights of an approaching car in a wooded clearing. Her brain flushed with the terrifying thought: 'Had the people who kidnapped her been associated with Lynden Brace?' Millie shivered at the thought.

"I'm sorry," said Lynden

"You must be getting chilly," he smiled.

"I'm afraid I had the gas disconnected a while back, so that iron monstrosity doesn't actually work anymore," he said pointing at the gas fire beneath the mantelpiece. Lynden rose to his feet. Millie smiled silently.

"Hang on there though, I'll go and see if I can rustle up some candles and blankets from the ottoman in the dining room." Lynden made his way across the sculptured dusky pink

168

carpet towards the archway between the living room and the dining area.

Night had fallen outside and the neighbouring room was in pitch darkness. Lynden turned in the shadows and walked back towards the living room, carrying a couple of soft woollen throws. Millie froze with fear as she watched the sinister shadow moving towards her. She nearly cried out in terror when she recognised the familiar gait of the figure standing in the archway. She would not allow herself to believe what she was thinking, 'Lynden Brace moved just like one of the kidnappers.'

The sudden look of terror on the teenager's face told Lynden all he needed to know. The master of illusion had been unmasked. Millie sprang up from the sofa and ran towards the front door. Her trembling hands reached for the latch. But her attempt to open the door was in vain as the controlling mentalist had double locked it earlier. Millie was trapped.

Lynden ran over to the door and ripped one of the pink tasselled curtain tie-backs off the wall by the window. He wrenched Millie's weak wrists behind her back, securing them with the scratchy pink cord. Millie began to scream, but Lynden slapped her hard across the face, frog-marched her across the room and pushed her back down onto the sofa.

"You stupid bitch," he hissed.

Millie slumped into the floral patterned cushions. Her face stung hard by the sudden smack. Heavy salty tears welled up in the terrified teenager's eyes. She swallowed hard and summoned every ounce of strength in her body to ask Lynden a trembling question.

"Why? What have I ever done to you?"

Lynden spun around to face his quarry. His eyes were aflame with anger.

"Why? Why?" he bellowed.

"I'll tell you fucking why shall I? Because your mother ruined my life, that's why." Millie stared back in silent terror.

"Your mother Carol Frogson was the fuckin' fraudulent waste of space who killed my sister," he spat as he stood up from the settee.

"She sponged thousands of pounds out of Poppy whilst filling her head with all that life after death bollocks. Your fuckin' mother scammed so much dosh out of my desperate broken-hearted sister that she was able to run away and start a whole new life with the proceeds. Once Carol fuckin' Frogson had wormed enough money out of Poppy she did a runner from that drug-peddling loser of a husband of hers; a nasty piece of shit who incidentally was your real dad!" Millie looked startled by this new revelation about her biological father.

"Your bitch of a mother was a long con artist; a cold-hearted gleaner who soaked up any facet of information about a person that she could get her hands on; anything that could be useful later on. She wound up Poppy so tight with her twisted lies and tricks." Millie remained silent; salty tears streamed down her hot face as Lynden Brace continued to unleash his tirade.

"When that fat old hag had sponged enough money from her scam, she needed to finish the job once and for all. But before she could run away to start a new life in the country she had to sever any links with her squalid past. So she set about convincing Poppy that Uncle Graham and baby Abi were waiting for her on the other side; she goaded her into believing that all she had to do was kill herself to be reunited with them," Lynden paced around the room, pausing every now and then, before turning to fire a steely glare at Millie. The terrified teenager stared back at him.

"Do you know how it feels to have everything taken away from you when you're fucking thirteen years old? he screamed; a burning pain fizzed through his heart.

"We were only fucking thirteen years old," he cried.

Lynden Brace was out of control. For the first time since that fateful day of discovering Poppy's lifeless body he had no plan, he had no practised responses, no pre-planned scenarios. Telling Millie that he and his brother had made it their life's mission to avenge their sister's death had never been part of the plan. Now the uncharted situation that was unfolding before his eyes was an alien concept for the mind controlling mentalist. He began to panic.

"You think my mom killed your loopy sister?" screamed Millie incredulously.

"So that's what you meant in the church today when you said that Cellestra had influenced your life so much that it moulded you into the monster you are today." Millie's deliberate misquotation of his eulogy grated on Lynden's nerves.

"All along you weren't being nice, you were just trying to be clever while venting your anger as you stood next to my mother's dead body. You weren't giving a heart-felt speech, you were just being a cold, callous calculating bastard trying to get revenge for your mental sister's suicide," she spat.

Lynden raised his hand and swiped it hard across Millie's face. But the defiant teenager wasn't about to lose the opportunity of telling him exactly how she felt.

"Maybe my mother was trying to give your weak deluded sibling the courage to move on, but it was your half-baked stupid wet sister who took that to mean she should end her own life," she jeered, the stinging in her face grew numb.

"Shut up. Shut up. Shut the fuck up! You spoilt little brat," he commanded. The magma of anger that had built in the pit of his stomach now raged through Lynden's body and erupted with the full force of a volcano searing through his veins. His taught right fist crunched into the delicate jaw line beneath Millie's wispy blonde hair, knocking her sideways off the sofa. Her motionless body lay at his feet, slumped on the dusky pink sculptured carpet.

"I should have let Kyle have his filthy fun with you in the factory when he had the chance," he wheezed.

#

Richens and Duke were in their car speeding through a maze of unfamiliar busy roads towards Dooley Croft. A small squadron of blue flashing lights and sirens had snaked behind the detectives' vehicle for the past eighty miles. Duke had contacted the northern police to ask they apprehend Bryan Cedel and secure the Manchester terraced home before they arrived. But his request had been denied. The local force's resources were severely stretched and, with no firm evidence of a crime being committed, their senior officer would not sanction

171

his officers to attend. The best he could offer was to ask a patrol car to pass by the road to take a look. Richens and Duke were locked in the same thought that neither of them dared to admit: They believed that Lynden Brace was going to kill Millie Moon; they only hoped to God they were not too late.

Trudi Jones' thorough background report of the Cedel family had unlocked many secrets of the two brothers' lives. With the help of psychologists and a small profiling team, the ambitious young officer had managed to build up an accurate picture of how the Cedel twins had coped following the untimely death of Phillipa Harrison. Richens and Duke had not known the brothers firmly blamed Carol Frogson for the death of their sister.

A few years after Poppy's suicide Bryan and Kyle Cedel realised Carol had successfully reinvented herself. She had conveniently forgotten the squalid scamming life that she had led with Peter Frogson and she had begun to successfully ply her trade with a new name, Cellestra Moon. That was the catalyst that had set the brothers firmly on the road to revenge. Kyle Cedel had tried to bring Cellestra's empire down on the internet with his trolling attempts, but that hadn't worked. Kyle was the less cautious of the two brothers and he had never thought his actions through properly. Getting caught for trolling was careless. Filling his head with an overdose of fantasy and science fiction films had almost re-wired his brain; he had totally lost his grip on reality. The virtual world he had created as StarBoy had become real life for Kyle Cedel. He had begun to feel he was invincible. The immature troll had never imagined he would get caught out so easily.

While he was serving his sentence for cyber abuse, Kyle had decided he would need help to bring down Cellestra Moon; someone publicly unconnected with him who he could deflect the blame onto should anything go wrong. After his release from prison he had cast his net by speaking on the phone-in radio show; the ambitious Rosie Carmichael had been more than eager to swallow his bait. But Kyle Cedel always failed to think things through. At the end of the Cellestragate affair, the vengeful twin had gained nothing. All his escapade had achieved was to give the fake Psychic heightened publicity, which in turn had simply bolstered her popularity. But at least he'd managed to remain fairly anonymous in that particular fiasco and Rosie Carmichael had been the one left to take the flack.

In contrast to his brother, the calculating mentalist Bryan Cedel had spent many years formulating and honing his plan. He too had invented a whole new persona to hide behind. After the brothers had been taken into care, following the death of their sister, they had eventually been fostered out to two separate families. Bryan had been particularly relieved to escape the shackles of being one half of the Twingers. His well-to-do foster family were keen members of an amateur dramatics society and they encouraged him to follow his dream of a stage career. Bryan relished the new lease of life and quickly embraced a future in the theatre; honing his skills as an actor, a magician and compelling showman. Unknown to the outside world, Bryan Cedel had plotted all along to reap his revenge on Carol Frogson. He had patiently waited for seventeen long years, ironing out every single scenario, developing his skills and building his reputation whilst re-planning and re-thinking every possible outcome. He had dissected every minute detail, until that fateful night just over two weeks ago, when it had become time for this calculating predator to strike.

DI Richens raced his car along the road. Duke noticed his boss was deep in thought. He was biting hard on his bottom lip and gripping the steering wheel firmly in both hands. He dutifully followed the orders occasionally barked at him from a Sat-Nav, as the car snaked through miles of narrow country lanes. Duke's mind flashed back to the image of Rosie Carmichael's lifeless strangled body. There had already been enough deaths associated with this case and both men were determined that Millie Moon was not going to become another statistic.

"I felt a bit sorry for Rosie Carmichael though sir," muttered Duke, trying to break the tense silence in the car.

"She had obviously got it in for Kyle Cedel and wanted her revenge for the havoc he had caused in her life," continued the Sergeant.

"I just think it's such a waste of talent, a great investigative mind like that and she totally blows it by killing him," Richens looked across at Duke quizzically.

"Investigative mind? Pha!" snorted Richens.

"She was just a dozy crack head who got lucky Duchess," he added dismissively.

While Rosie Carmichael had been sat in the CID office answering all of Richens' questions about Cellestragate, she had managed to read one of the upside-down names printed at the top of one of the manila folders that had fallen from Duke's grasp onto the desk. Rosie realised the MagicMan pseudonym had been circled in red which suggested to her it was important and would probably have some relation to Cellestra Moon. Her inquisitive mind had worked overtime that evening and it didn't take very long for Rosie to track down MagicMan through a sci-fi forum. Pretty soon she had struck up a geeky conversation with him through the site using well-placed references to his favourite fantasy film. The forensic examination of Rosie's laptop revealed that she had managed to capture Kyle Cedel's email address from a private chat room in the forum. Armed with that small snippet of seemingly innocuous information, Rosie had researched his email address online and had soon discovered him to be a regular member of the Sci-Fi-Dater dating website. Rosie's carefully chosen and cleverly named alter-ego Magician's Assistant, had been the perfect bait to snare her hapless victim; she was simply too tempting for Kyle Cedel to resist. The forensic examination of Kyle Cedel's laptop and social media account revealed how he and his ideal woman had arranged to meet at his new bed-sit.

"The stupid cow should have told us as soon as she'd put two-and-two together instead of buggering off on a one woman crusade to reap her revenge and lure him to his death," continued Richens. Duke stared out at the front gardens and lamp posts speeding past his car window as Richens continued to drive aggressively along the winding suburban streets.

"Yes," agreed Duke, a pained expression returned to his tired face.

"Maybe then we could have intercepted her on her way to Kyle Cedel's bed-sit; or even picked her up before she put herself in danger."

"What beats me though sir is why Rosie switched Cedel's pay-as-you-go burner phone back on before she left his bed-sit?"

Richens smiled at Duke.

"Ah, that's easy," revealed Richens.

"She went to visit Kyle Cedel fully intending to kill him. She didn't want there to be anything to place her at the scene, so she left her own phone at home, just in case we'd be able to get any tracking data off it to prove she'd been in the area at the time of the troll's murder." Duke looked at his boss, with a slightly quizzical expression.

"I still don't get it though?"

"Well, after Rosie had pumped Kyle full of all the shit she had in her bag, she was quite understandably agitated and needed to score more heroin for herself," explained Richens.

"She must have tried to use Kyle's normal phone to call her crack dealer to get another supply but it had been turned off and was locked. The burner phone, which must have been next to it in Cedel's bed-sit, didn't have a lock on it so she used that one instead. She simply forgot to switch the phone off again afterwards."

"But wouldn't that be a bit of a risk sir," queried Duke.

"Surely she'd know we'd eventually trace the number that was called and the dealer would probably want to save his own skin and give us her name? Also her prints would place her at the scene?"

"Yeah, but she wasn't thinking straight was she Duchess, she probably thought we'd assume Cedel had made the call himself," replied Richens.

"All she had in her mind was to arrange a deal without using her own mobile. She'd just killed her Nemesis. I mean would you be in the right state of mind if you'd just done that?"

Richens' Sat-Nav rudely interrupted the two officers' conversation to announce there was one final turn in the road before they reached their destination. The car slowed and Richens switched off the headlights. Richens and Duke pulled

175

up outside the neat row of modest terraced houses in Dooley Croft. Their entourage of uniformed officers had switched off their blue lights and sirens a couple of miles back down the road. Richens had insisted a silent approach would give them all the best possible chance of apprehending Bryan Cedel by using the element of surprise.

"It certainly makes you think what a small world it is though Duchess," said Richens as he turned off the engine of his car.

"We've got intel that the name of the bloke Dozy Rosie called from Cedel's phone is none other than Peter Frogson." Duke stared back at his boss in astonishment.

"Peter Frogson is dealing drugs again?" questioned Duke.

"I thought he'd moved higher up the food chain since he was released from clink," he added dismissively. Richens raised his eyebrows and nodded his head.

"Yep, if the local snitch is to be believed it appears he's back dealing the Columbian party powder again Duchess, but more importantly it makes me wonder if he was the one who first gave the junkie bint the heads up on his ex-wife Carol in the first place?"

Chapter 17

Lynden Brace sat on the living room carpet gently stroking Millie's swollen face. She lay unconscious on the floor, her head cradled in his lap.

"Where did it all go wrong Millie?" he whispered into her ear as he gently rocked back and forth on the floor. He was trying to methodically work through the scenario; to work out where it had all become unravelled; how he could somehow get it all back on track; take back control.

Lynden Brace's clever plan to bring about the ultimate downfall of the country's most adored Medium had meant he had no alternative but to enlist the help of his estranged brother. Lynden needed to take advantage of the fact that Kyle was the slightly more effeminate of the two brothers; it would be so much easier for Kyle to pass himself off as a woman. Lynden had selected his brother's disguise carefully. A long raincoat would cover any clothing worn beneath. A red curly wig would be a fine fitting tribute to the memory of their long-dead flame-haired sister. Lynden had picked up a pair of rose tinted glasses. They would serve as a clever last-minute twist that would see Kyle blend in effortlessly with the rest of Cellestra's delusional adoring crowd. Lynden Brace had instructed his brother to find a willing accomplice to steal one of Crucible's cars and drive the mini cab to the studio car park. Kyle had dutifully arranged for one of his desperate fellow transient boarders at the bed and breakfast to act as a driver. The promise of a few hundred pounds for simply grabbing, gagging and dropping off a teenager proved too much of a temptation for the greasy alcoholic ex-mechanic to resist.

All Lynden needed to do next was to arrange for VIP invitations to a local author's book launch to be sent to Millie and her wannabe friends. The pull of a celebrity party would be too great for the excitable social climber to resist. Lynden knew that Cellestra and her daughter argued constantly and it would only be a matter of time before the petulant teenager would flounce out of the studios and try to storm off in her car, determined to attend the celebrity bash. On the day of the kidnapping Kyle's new recruit had quickly disabled the engine of Millie's car by disconnecting its high tension lead so it wouldn't start. He had then simply sat back in his stolen taxi cab and waited for her to stomp out of the stage door as Lynden had confidently predicted she would.

With a text from the greasy mechanic to say Millie was safely restrained in the back of his car, Kyle Cedel had handed over the package at Cellestra's meet and greet session later that evening, before slipping down a service corridor towards the dressing rooms. Lynden had told him exactly where the CCTV blind spots were; especially the perfectly sheltered square metre zone where he could swiftly take off the rose-tinted glasses undetected, change his wig for a short black one and remove his raincoat to reveal a trademark Navy blue suit underneath. The next camera would catch the back of him entering the toilets. There he carefully applied a false goatee beard and emerged from the toilets exposing a purple silk waistcoat with matching perfectly knotted tie and a very pale pink silk shirt. Anyone viewing the grainy black and white footage would at first glance simply assume it was Lynden Brace coming and going about his business at the studios. The mentalist calculated there was a small chance that the video footage would be viewed by one of Hanford's more observant police officers, and they may notice the mysterious woman disappear into thin air at the CCTV blind spot and seemingly emerge as Lynden Brace on the other side. Although he was never questioned by the police, Lynden had made sure he had a water-tight alibi to prove he was nowhere near the studios at the time. He would have simply suggested the person must have been an impostor trying to implicate him in the kidnapping if he had ever been challenged.

"It was a beautiful plan Millie," whispered Lynden.

"If only your fucking low-life mother had been honest and told everyone the truth in the first place. If only she'd have owned up to the fact that she was a fucking money-grabbing fat bitch who lied and scammed her way through life, preying on innocent people, none of this circus would have happened." Lynden continued to rock back and forth on the floor.

178

"If only she had followed my simple instruction to get David to buy the ticket instead of brazenly going into a corner shop and buying it herself."

#

Richens and Duke stood on the driveway in front of 7 Dooley Croft. The over-grown front garden led to a panelled front door. Heavy curtains hung at the bay window and Richens could just make out a feint glint of lamplight in the crack between where the two heavy floral curtains met at the middle. He motioned to four of the uniformed officers to guard the front door, before he and Duke made their way quietly to the back of the house. The rear moonlit garden lay mostly in darkness as Richens and Duke stumbled slowly through the over-grown weeds towards the kitchen door. Richens swore under his breath as he unexpectedly caught the edge of his calf on a large sand-filled plant pot. The planter had been placed on the paving slabs by the back door; a small collection of cigarette stubs had been pushed into the sand and neatly arranged in a circle inside.

"Damn smokers," winced Richens as his leg began to throb. The two men stopped and waited for a few moments to make sure no one inside the house had heard them arrive. After a couple of minutes, Richens hesitantly placed his hand on the kitchen door handle, drew in a deep breath and pressed down slowly to try the latch. Unexpectedly the door clicked open and began to swing towards a glass fronted kitchen display cabinet. Richens swiftly grabbed the aluminium frame of the door to stop it from moving too quickly in the breeze and to prevent it banging open onto the cupboard behind. He turned to Duke and raised his index finger to his lips to signal he needed silent back-up from his Sergeant.

The two men slowly entered the kitchen and made their way over towards the panelled wooden door on the opposite side of the room. They could clearly hear a man's voice from behind the other side of the door. It was Lynden Brace.

"Did you know your fucking bitch of a mother managed to conveniently re-package her whole life, as if Carol Frogson had never existed," ranted Lynden.

179

"Her wall of memories in her dressing room held no tributes to her former life. They just started from the day she became the joke that was Cellulite Moo," he hissed.

"Just like that," Lynden snapped his fingers angrily.

"She had forgotten Carol Frogson, as conveniently as she had forgotten she had killed my sister Poppy." Millie stirred slightly and tried to open her eyes.

"How many more innocent people did your nasty vindictive bitch of a mother deceive and then forget about? Hmm?" Lynden kept on relentlessly rocking back and forth; Millie's head bumping and bouncing in his lap.

"That manipulative sow wasn't afraid for your safety Emily, all those years of over-bearing smothering. She wasn't doing that for your benefit," he snorted.

"Oh no, she knew that one day her filthy dirty past would catch up with her and bite her on her stinking fat arse so hard that she would never feel anything again except pain." Millie winced as her fractured jaw caught the side of Lynden's leg.

"Your mommy dearest was more worried about losing her reputation than the safety of her own daughter."

"She was a coward Millie, a fucking pissed-up coward. She couldn't even face up to living with herself after she did the decent thing by confessing to me that she was a fraud. She had to go and fucking top herself," he laughed.

"Did they tell you how I found her?" he goaded cruelly.

"The odorous mountain of blubber foaming at the mouth in her dressing room? Her grasping pudding fingers couldn't get the cap off her bottle of brandy quickly enough," he recalled gaily.

"And then she'd shovelled every last one of those pills down her fat throat until she choked," he laughed as Millie's head bounced up and down on his lap again. Richens and Duke stood silently behind the door to the living room, waiting for the right moment.

"The only thing I hadn't banked on was you escaping Emily," said Lynden coldly as he playfully twirled the other pink cord curtain tie-back through his fingers.

"Did you like my bit of acting there back at the factory? I learned how to change my voice at stage school you know," he announced proudly. A familiar sinister tone flooded each word. "It was a beautiful plan Emily, it took me ages to get everything just right. At the end that stupid waste of air Kyle was supposed to kill you once he'd finished with you. Did you know that?" he snorted.

"But oh no, instead he had to celebrate when he heard your fat joke of a mother had killed herself. Not only did my masterful plan go right out of the window but, rather than kill you as planned, the wanking ginger cretin was more interested in shagging that dozy journalist who'd tracked him down on the internet," shouted Lynden incredulously.

"He should have been there at the factory finishing you off whilst I was standing guard over Cellulite Moo's fat blubbering corpse." Lynden had slipped the cord tie-back around Millie's neck and was gently pulling the tassel through the end loop to form a noose.

"And then today at the churchyard, you just couldn't help yourself could you. You had to spoil it all by saying you and that bastard David Moon were going to re-ignite the whole fucking scam again, bring it full circle and take over where your stinking fat sow of a mother left off." Millie's big blue eyes stared up at him. Frozen with fear, she was unable to cry out through the pain of her broken teeth.

"That snivelling waste of air Kyle always was unpredictable," continued Lynden slowly tugging at the cord.

"He never thought things through." Lynden's mind began to race.

"I was on my way over to see him last week when that dozy reporter turned up, dressed up to the nines all ready to eat Kyle for breakfast," his voice getting harder now.

"But I couldn't run the risk you see Emily. I knew he'd probably blabbed about everything to her in exchange for a quick lick of her tits, so she had to be dealt with."

"That wanker never could follow simple instructions. Why would he never learn that I was the one who made the plans? I was the one who thought things through. He was just a glorified errand boy. All he had to do was stick to the plan. How the fuck

181

could we ever have been related?" Lynden's thoughts appeared to wander off momentarily.

"So I'm afraid I had to follow Reporter Rosie home," he smiled inwardly at the memory of the terror he had seen in the green eyes of the bewildered young woman as she took her last fretful gulp of air.

"I had to kill her Emily . . . just like I'm going to have to kill you."

Millie felt the oxygen leave her lungs; unable to take another breath she began to choke, her body twisting on the dusky pink carpet as Richens and Duke burst into the room.

"What? You're going to kill Millie just like that shit-for-brains reporter killed your brother?" screamed Richens. DS Duke ran across the living room floor and threw his body onto Lynden Brace. Millie rolled to one side as the two men grappled on the floor. A scrum of shouting uniformed PCs flooded into the living room and joined in the foray to finally overpower the mentalist. Richens watched DS Duke pull Lynden Brace's arms firmly behind his back and snap a set of handcuffs securely into place. A couple of female police officers helped a dazed Millie to her feet.

"That Rosie Carmichael held a serious grudge against your brother didn't she Bryan?" Lynden turned to face the breathless Inspector.

"What the hell do you mean?" he spat.

"Your brother Kyle Cedel, the StarBoy MagicMan Casey who hounded Cellestra Moon for years on the internet," replied Richens wheezing.

"My brother? What the fucking hell are you talking about?" protested Lynden. Millie turned towards him.

"You fucking know who he's talking about, you bastard," slurred Millie as blood began to pour from her mouth.

"That stupid waste of space Kyle who never thought things through," she spluttered, wriggling free of a supportive female police officer's grasp. Millie summoned every last ounce of strength in her body to launch herself at Lynden. With one swift kick, her right knee met him firmly in the crotch as her right hand slapped hard across his flushed face. Duke let Lynden fall to the floor gasping for air.

"That's for my fucking mother, you creepy bastard," she hissed, a shower of blood spitting from Millie's mouth rained down on his face. As Lynden groaned on the floor DI Richens cleared his throat before reading out his caution.

"Bryan Neil Cedel, also known as Lynden Brace, I'm arresting you for the kidnapping and attempted murder of Millie Moon, formerly known as Emily Frogson; I'm also arresting you on suspicion of false imprisonment, fraud and extortion. Also for the suspected manslaughter of Cellestra Moon; the murder of Rosie Carmichael, the suspected murder of an as yet unidentified white male found in Witches' Wood. You do not have to say anything, but it may harm your defence if you do not mention when questioned something which you later rely on in court. Anything you do say may be given in evidence. Do you understand?" Lynden remained crouched on the floor, writhing in agony and crying.

"If I had my way you'd also be under arrest for the crime against fashion by wearing such dreadfully pretentious coloured waistcoats," muttered Richens under his breath, as he and Duke dragged Bryan Cedel out into the moon-lit street and into a waiting police car.

Chapter 18

Three months later

The Granary Mill Hotel was a mock Tudor building at the end of a long tree-lined driveway. The grounds had once been part of the Himley Estate and its owners had capitalised on this tenuous link to re-brand it as being part of a stately home. The hotel was conveniently located at the edge of Hanford town and it was a popular location for local business executives to visit when meeting clients. It was a moderately sized hotel that offered a certain degree of anonymity for its guests yet it still retained a warm homely atmosphere. The private nooks and crannies in the residents' bar were privy to the hushed secrets of many business deals; the medieval wooden booths kept thousands of covert conversations totally confidential.

A soft autumn breeze cooled Millie's face as she quickly made her way through the entrance doors and into the wooden beamed foyer. A tall, lean gentleman with short cropped blonde hair immediately stood up to greet her. He was a good looking man in his late-forties, but his leathery tanned complexion made him look slightly older. He wore a well-tailored yet simple pale blue linen suit with a tasteful plain white silk shirt. His whole demeanour understated his power and wealth.

"Hello Emily. It's so lovely to meet you." Peter Frogson awkwardly stepped forward to embrace his daughter. Millie smiled warmly and gave him a hesitant kiss on the cheek.

"Thank you for agreeing to see me," she replied.

Following Cellestra's death, David had felt it only right to reveal everything to Millie about her biological father. He had hoped that having no secrets between them would help him to re-build their fragile relationship. But Millie was finding it impossible to forgive him for lying to her for most of her life. The man she had always looked up to and loved as a father had helped her selfish mother to reinvent their family unit. Their wicked lies now meant Millie felt she didn't really know who she was any more. David had explained Cellestra only ever wanted to protect her daughter from the squalid life she had escaped from; but the young woman had hundreds of questions that David simply had no answers for. She believed she had a right to know her real father and needed to hear the story from both sides. Her only route to the truth behind her mother's deception had been to track down Peter Frogson.

Millie followed Peter through the hotel foyer and into the residents' bar. They sat down in a cosy wooden booth beneath a large stained glass window, as a waitress quickly skipped over to the table to take their drinks order.

"You look quite a bit like your mum used to when she was younger," said Peter in an attempt to break the silence. Millie smiled back, unsure whether it was a genuine compliment or just a statement of fact.

When Millie was first told about her biological father she had at first been confused and then angry; but over the months she had developed a great sadness and regret that she had never known Peter Frogson existed. Even if he had been the drug-peddling waste of space that David described him as, Millie believed she should have been told the truth earlier; she should have been allowed to make her own choice about whether to have any contact with him or not. Her mother had no right to make that decision for her and cut him out of her life completely.

A waiter arrived with a fresh cafetiere of coffee, two bone China cups and a small jug of cream and placed them on the table. Millie watched and silently took in every detail. Peter politely thanked the young man and asked him if the hotel had any Turbinado sugar as he preferred it to Demerara. The waiter smiled back and said he would ask the bar manager. Millie was pleasantly surprised. The man sat in front of her was well-dressed, elegant, charming and seemingly well-educated; he bore no resemblance to the low-life loser that David had described.

"So Emily . . ." he paused, his deep blue eyes met her thoughtful gaze.

". . . or should I call you Millie?"

"Whatever you're happy with," she smiled, warming to him.

"Okay, Millie it is then. And you must call me Pete . . . I think calling me Dad would be rather alien to both of us." Millie poured out two cups of coffee and offered the cream to her father. The waiter returned with a small silver dish of Turbinado cane sugar and Peter promptly put a spoonful into his china cup.

"Sorry about being so picky about the sugar," he explained.

"It's just I got a taste for it when I was in South America once." Millie raised her eyebrows in surprise. He was evidently well-travelled as well.

"Wow, what were you doing there?" she asked.

"Oh not much really; just a short business trip," he replied, almost dismissively. Peter was keen to drop the small talk and steer the conversation towards a much more delicate topic. It was time to stop ignoring the elephant in the room.

"I suppose you're sitting there expecting me to say Carol was a nasty and vindictive bitch for grassing me up all those years ago." Millie was surprised by the swift change in subject.

"Truth be told, back then, your mum was as much a key player in the dope-pedalling operation as I was." The young girl felt a small shock of pins and needles tingle in her heart at the revelation of another secret from her mother's carefully edited past.

"Yes, it was cruel of her to cut off all contact with me, but you mustn't only blame your mother" he continued as he picked up his coffee cup and blew across the top to cool its contents slightly.

"In a funny sort of way I guess she did me a favour really. It made me turn my life around into the man I am today. I probably couldn't have done any of it with a kid in tow." He took a sip of hot coffee and savoured the caramel flavoured liquid on his tongue, aware that he had probably sounded a little cavalier regarding his fatherly responsibilities.

Millie assumed his slightly abrupt tone was a coping mechanism. How else could anyone regard their child being taken away from them as a blessing in disguise? She chose to believe he had probably been in denial. She imagined that during many cold dark nights in his prison cell, he must have convinced himself that never seeing his little girl again was for the best; she would be better off without him. That defence had been the only way he had managed to get through all those difficult years alone. It was the best explanation Millie could come up with as to how her biological father had found it so easy to cope with the prospect of never seeing her again.

The slightly awkward meeting unexpectedly blossomed into a pleasant afternoon for the estranged father and daughter. Millie left no stone unturned as she delivered a full resume of her cosseted life and the stifling bubble of lies and secrets that had enveloped her world. Finally she relaxed back in her seat and listened intently to her father's story.

Peter explained that after finishing his prison sentence he vowed never to place a foot inside Her Majesty's Hell hole again. A friend on the outside had given him a job as a delivery driver. After a couple of years he proved himself to be so indispensable to the business that he was given another position with more responsibility. Pretty soon he began to climb a precarious career ladder in buying and selling. He successfully fought his way out of poverty and was adamant he would never go back to the squalid life he had known with Carol. With the job promotion came the opportunity to build and nurture his own lucrative client base. When his friend passed away, Peter seized the opportunity to take over the firm. He was now a moderately successful businessman, earning a modest income with a generally happy life. He neglected to tell Millie that the commodity his business had been involved in distributing was Cocaine.

At the end of their meeting Millie stood up and gave her father a warm heartfelt goodbye hug. It had been a pleasant afternoon and she hoped it would be the first of many. She reached into her handbag and pulled out a small piece of pale pink paper that had been folded into four and safely stored in a zipped up pocket inside. Hesitantly she bit her bottom lip.

"Before I leave I want you to have this," she said, quickly passing it to him. Peter took the slip of paper from her hand and unfolded it. He was shocked to discover it was a winning lottery ticket; it was the one David Moon had bought after Lynden Brace's Fool The Nation programme had been recorded. Peter was speechless. He had hoped for a small memento to mark the first meeting with his daughter in over seventeen years; a photograph perhaps. This was absolutely the last thing he had expected.

"Dad . . . err I mean David," faltered Millie. She took in a deep breath, annoyed that she still hadn't managed to break the habit of a lifetime referring to Cellestra's husband in that way.

"David doesn't know I have it. I stole it out of his safe. He doesn't deserve the money anyway, what with all the income he's getting off book and film deals about Cellestra's life and the royalties from the 'I Can See You' documentary. The lottery ticket is filthy money and I don't want to have anything to keep reminding me of that totally dreadful episode. It was absolutely the worst time of my life." Millie's mind momentarily drifted back to the petrifying week she had spent held captive in the factory unit.

"I've been thinking about the cruel way my mother cut you off all those years ago. I don't want the ticket, David isn't worthy of it. So, after finally meeting you today, it seems only fitting that you should have it. Call it compensation if you like for missing out on the trappings of Cellestra's success. Maybe you could put some of it towards another trip to South America," added Millie. She kissed him one last time on the cheek and walked out of the residents' bar; happy that she had done the right thing.

Peter quickly placed the precious piece of paper inside his wallet, pulled a twenty pound note out of the bill fold and left it on the table to cover the cost of the afternoon coffees. A broad smile grew across his leathery tanned face as he briskly walked outside onto the car park. Today had been an unexpectedly good day. He stood by his car, took a pack of cigarettes out of his jacket pocket and fumbled in one of his trouser pockets searching for his trusty lighter. He raised a cigarette to his lips and flicked the familiar mauve coloured lighter into life. He inhaled hard and laughed at the well-worn logo printed on the side of the lighter; a gold-coloured top hat with 'Brace Yourself' written in black print beneath. He cleared his throat with a small cough and smiled. Today had been a very good day indeed for Peter Frogson.

THE END

Printed in Great Britain
by Amazon

28683331R00106